KARIMA'S JOURNEY
BACK TO AFRICA

A. Yvonne Stokes

CHARMED LIFE BOOKS

For information address Charmed Life Club Books, a division of Charmed Life Publishing Inc. P.O. Box 777906 Henderson, NV 89077

Cover design: Charmed Life Club Artworks

ISBN-978-1-7359697-1-8

Library of Congress Control Number: TXu2-217-250
First Printed in the United States of America

Dedicated to the children of the diaspora;
may we come to know who we are and present accordingly.

PART ONE

We Had Our Day

CHAPTER 1

Karima

Isn't it ironic that we acquire wisdom later in life when our energy, fearlessness and beauty are waning? In other words, those attributes aren't in play at the same time when we know more than we have ever known before. I want to find a way to beat that paradox by slowing father time down so I can make my acquired wisdom work for me now during my second act.

Looking at myself in the bathroom mirror, I see an attractive, and from some angles, sexy middle-aged woman. I've been fighting hard to keep my fifty-five year old self tight and it has paid off, but here I am picking at the flaws I can find, covering the gray in my temples and my eyebrows with a few strokes of mascara - I make that bad boy do double duty. I was feeling pretty good about myself for a minute as I gazed at my reflection, inspecting myself.

I looked around and admired my low budget, DIY tub tiling project. Some people think you can't lay wall tile without experience, but I had done it with different shades of off white in differing textures and shapes and it was stunning if I had to say so myself. My cell phone buzzed on the sink, almost vibrating over the edge with a text - it was from my friend at the office - warning me that the boss was already in and was asking where I was. Daggone, I'm late again, I said to myself. I felt guilty for a second and then turned cocky – I know why I'm so complacent, I'm not motivated to be on time. Why rush in to do the same thing every day, be made to kowtow to people less educated, not hardly as intelligent or witty as I am, who I am learning nothing from and who all sit around waiting for that once in a blue moon sale to close.

I worked at a thriving real estate office in downtown Phoenix where I felt tolerated at best. I was a successful agent, but never got the big listings. I had recently been demoted to residential rentals, but I was still doing well and outperforming my competition. Clients liked my direct, matter of fact manner and my trustworthy character I was told. I was the only black female in the pool of agents. I did all the right things to move up fast. I read classic sales books, took advantage of every seminar offered by management, attended conferences and so forth, but I never advanced. Not one to cry discrimination easily, I chalked it up to my age since most of my "colleagues" were young and tech savvy. In the back of my mind though, I remembered when a co-worker asked me about the wigs feigning curiosity about how often one needed to wash and style them. I pretended not to get the insult and answered the question as though it were legitimate, but I was crushed, especially because I did regularly wash and style them. I looked in the restroom mirror that day and saw what they saw, an over-weight, wig wearing, makeup free Black woman with moles. I got it, but I didn't *get it*.

To redeem myself, I decided to stage a "reboot" which I had already been thinking about doing anyway. First though, I needed to settle on my new style. I loved the natural hair movement and the no make-up look that included make-up, but I also admired the polished matte look combined with straight hair and sharp angles. Magazines and YouTube videos were bound to help I thought. Releasing myself from the memories of that day weeks ago, I jumped into my 2003, red, five-speed BMW I called "Clutch," and headed to work.

Once I arrived at my cubicle seven minutes late, I was fired on the spot. It was handled very matter-of-factly by my direct report. Stone faced and solemn, I said thank you, placed my personal property into my large bag and walked out the door while the other agents leered and smirked at me in the background. I wasn't going to give them the satisfaction of seeing me cry or looking scared. I had a mind to sue the suckers or at least go the EEOC route, but figured the legitimate lateness issue, no matter the insignificance of the minutes, would justify their actions legally, so I said, "screw it" and let it go.

That was three weeks ago and I was now down to six thousand dollars to my name. I figure, at fifty-five, I can go ahead and get another menial job, or I can use my mind to figure out a better way. Thinking back on all the jobs I'd held through the years while raising my son, Hassan, I couldn't remember many joyful moments. My friend Allison, nicknamed, "Skanki," suggested I "get on the corner." We named her Skanki for a reason. That girl is so alive and fun.

I can't figure out why employers do either nothing or the absolute minimum to make work more rewarding and beneficial for employees in order to have a motivated, stable workforce. I figured that if workers enjoy their work, feel appreciated and valued, they will in turn do their best and be especially productive. I recalled the office-cleaning gig I had when Hassan was a toddler. I suggested that they dust and mop each night instead of weekly and was told to just do as I was instructed to do by the supervisor. That very next week, the cleaning company was released for inadequate performance. Instead of receiving a promotion or at least acknowledgement of my astute observations, my hours were reduced. Had they valued my insight, maybe they would have kept the contract. Just remembering that and many other frustrating experiences "on the job" made me realize I really didn't want another j-o-b.

Even though I don't have a degree beyond my associate's degree and have not worked in leadership positions, I am a reader and a thinker. I have thought of and abandoned many business ideas, but still believe that, miraculously, one of them will one day earn me a great salary and help somebody at the same time. I had nurtured ideas to create an interactive Black history website, a natural product nail salon for airports and a nationwide, elite "rite of passage" program for "children of the diaspora," the captured Africans turned slaves, to name a few. Before being tempted to find another empty job, I decided to ponder them all and think of a few more before making a decision on what to do because I couldn't afford to be unemployed much longer having no one to fall back on. I was grateful to God for the courage to consider taking risks at this stage in my life.

That didn't stop the pity party though. Bored, I called Skanki and decried the injustice in the world. We went on for a couple of hours *ad nauseum* about how people try to keep a 'sistah down before we admitted to each other that we shouldn't have been so willing to settle for mediocrity. Skanki said, "Girl, you 'shouda sued those fools. Here you are running circles around them other agents and they fire *you*!" I laughed and said, "You're right, I should have acted a fool in there and started turning over the desk and what not, but I wasn't trying to get arrested." "And you know this," Skanki replied. "Bottom line, they didn't want me there. I didn't fit in with the company brand anymore once they got under new ownership. I was playing myself anyway. I need to be in business for myself and get out from under the control of other people," I told Skanki. "Yeah, sometimes we stick out like a sore thumb on these jobs. Our culture is really different in many respects and it's really hard to fit in when you don't have that common cultural background and you look different from other folks. They don't even realize it, but they prefer people who look and act like them. Like sometimes you don't get their jokes and they don't get yours or they don't really try to get to know you once they've completed their cursory evaluation of your value," Skanki complained. I agreed and we finally got off the phone. Needing divine intervention, I got on my knees, said my prayers and made my requests for an opportunity known to the Lord.

CHAPTER 2

Spirit

With the assent of the Almighty, I have traversed the skies and the lands for hundreds of years from the time of Ancient Ethiopia, my beloved homeland. The Almighty blessed me to follow the lives of many of my descendants through countless generations, including my favoured Karima. The world had changed so much, but never seemed to learn from its past.

From my mother's womb, I was a curious child. Once I could safely run, I moved across the fields and lands adjacent to our village with my brothers, Kam and Johan, just for the joy of running. We had a sense of pride and completeness wrapped in the security of our family and the protection of our land. We could recount the names of our forefathers and mothers generations back without hesitation. We children helped out with the animals and crops and stayed out of the way of the adults, but we were made to feel special by the people of our village, called Homer.

Looking back, our food and clothing were simple but adequate. We valued each other, not things as people do in present times. The Elders of our village were given the highest respect and they upheld the rule of law. Africans believed in one God, the Supreme Being, and quarrels were resolved by the Elders in a democratic fashion based on equal rights of the villagers. Things began to change once we all moved North.

Before we left, I noticed how the parents talked amongst themselves with furrowed brows and alert eyes. I was playing in the dirt one morning and noticed my mother and father moving our things about. They looked forlorn and weary. Most of the other villagers started walking carrying their belongings on their heads. To my surprise, we joined them. We walked north night and day along the shore of the Red Sea for many days and many months until we reached the lands not far from the Mediterranean Sea. Only a child back then, I had no real sense of where we were or where we were going but, one day, we finally stopped walking. A few children and adults were lost along the way. Those of us children who made it, were ashen, exhausted and confused. We had no idea why we left our beloved land and homes in the first place.

A few days after we arrived, it became clear that this new land was very different from Homer. Where our landscape had been arid with few trees or plant life, this new land was green and lush. The temperature was warm, not hot, and the dirt bore crops and fruit effortlessly. The soil was moist and brown with red undertones instead of the color of dried clay, as I had known. The people looked like us, dark and long with expressive eyes, but they moved faster and talked more. The biggest change was all the structures. There were all kinds of places to go and to live in and they all looked different. My brother told me that the burial tombs were much bigger than the ones from our village and they contained so many more items to make life easier after death.

Even though we moved, we were all still devoted to using our earthly lives to prepare for the eternal afterlife, which is so different from modern times, the times of my beloved Karima. People of current times value life on earth and appear to give no thought at all to life after physical death.

CHAPTER 3

Karima

Now, having a lot of time on my hands, I hand washed "Clutch" and watered my plants. My mind wandered to my parents, Elliott and Mary, who had passed away within a year of each other when I was in my early thirties. They were both relatively young at the times of their deaths which were hastened by stressful lives laced with chronic poverty and unfulfilled dreams.

Elliott had caved to family pressure to drop out of college when Mary became pregnant with me. He thought it was the right thing to do as well since Mary had miscarried their first child, the unnamed son Elliott really wanted. Elliott and Mary licked their wounds, got married and reared me. Raised in the late sixties and seventies in inner city Los Angeles, I grew up along with my young, hip parents, who insisted I call them by their first names. Back then, blacks rarely got solid government or union jobs, so Elliott worked at grocery stores, clerking and cleaning. Mary was a trained classical pianist without an avenue to promote her work, so she served as a church musician to contribute towards the bills. Elliott loved us, but did not come to terms with leaving school. It never seemed to occur to him that he could re-enroll. Frustration and anger set in and I noticed that my parents argued more and more by the time I reached middle school. Creatures of their environment, Mary and Elliott eventually picked up bad habits, drinking and partying late into the night, often leaving me alone with my books and my dreams.

During that period of my childhood, I began to really think about the unfairness of my parents' situation. They were caught up in a set of circumstances not of their own making. On our small black and white television, I had seen the marches and speeches of our civil rights leaders when I was younger. Having been taught civics in school, I remember thinking, "If all people are equal under the law, why are blacks treated so differently?" It didn't make sense to me since blacks were the victims. Elliott was well read and was what people now call, "woke." He had talked to me about slavery and the African "diaspora," so I had an understanding of the past, which was a source of pride in our home. I was named for an Ancient Ethiopian village called, "Karima." My parents changed their surname before I was born from Jones to Powers reasoning that it offended their dignity and that of their ancestors to knowingly carry and pass down the surname of an oppressive slave owner who killed, brutalized and owned other human beings. Elliott would say, "You have to come up with a lot of bull to justify owning other people." In psychology, they call it "cognitive dissonance." Although Powers was also an English surname, they chose it because of its root word, power.

Still, despite possessing knowledge and pride, I watched my parents shrink, emotionally and physically. Elliott began to carry himself as though he were half a man. The liquor nor the partying could fill the void in their lives of who and what they were supposed to be. They managed to keep a roof over their heads and mine, but sometimes dinner was just a can of tuna between the three of us and maybe a few carrots or whatever was in the refrigerator. Life added another burden when their respective health conditions began to decline with Mary's diabetes diagnosis and Elliott's chronic high blood pressure. Both necessitated prescriptions they could not afford, so the conditions went uncontrolled.

My parents put all their hopes and dreams into me when I went to college. Even though it was a community college, they knew I would transfer to "the university," as they so proudly called it. In so doing, I would fulfill the dream of a college diploma for all of us in a sense. Consistent with the theme of our lives however, fate threw another curve ball. I met Hassan's father, Malcolm Barnes, a pretty boy/player or "jive sucker," as he was known in our household. I became pregnant on my only intimate encounter with him. He seemed to lose interest in me after that. Malcolm, learning of my pregnancy, tendered the classic doubts regarding paternity and "got ghost" real fast, playing only a token role in his son's life thereafter. My unplanned pregnancy deflated my family's collective hope for a diploma from "the university," but nine months later came a reprieve from the misery upon the birth of Hassan Jabron Powers.

Hassan's birth brought immeasurable joy and pleasure to the family and Elliott finally got his boy. Elliott taught Hassan to play basketball when the child was three years old. He took him to the barbershop and trained him to take out the trash, apparently a must when raising a boy. Hassan's every move was photographed and documented until Elliott's fatal heart attack when Hassan was ten years old. Mary, overcome with grief, passed away from complications of a stroke a year after Elliott's death. After that, Hassan became my lifeline, my reason for living. Without any family support, I hunkered down emotionally to do the job of mother and a father for my son. I didn't trust men enough to date after the trauma and embarrassment of my first romantic liaison. A college dropout at that point, I took on a variety of menial jobs throughout Hassan's childhood to get by and had thought my last one as a real estate agent would be my career and give me the financial security I craved, to no avail.

As a single mother, I had been through a lot and sacrificed to raise a decent human being. I didn't think I deserved a prize, I just knew that I could have done things differently and thought more about my wants and desires. In hindsight, I respect the decisions I made back then because they bore fruit.

I fondly recalled the time I used my treasured dime collection to take Hassan to Disneyland. What a time we had arriving at the park when it opened and staying until closing. Hassan was eleven at the time and wanted to ride every roller coaster and everything that simulated driving. I originally intended to use the dimes to buy a special perfume for myself, but decided instead to treat my son, still somber after the deaths of his grandparents. Don't get me wrong though, there was a time when I wanted to join Skanki out there in the clubs. She told me I was going to "dry up and die" if I didn't get out there and get my freak on. A part of me wanted to join her and be crazy, but I couldn't leave my son with people I didn't know that well so I could have some fun. Years later, Skanki told me she was glad I hadn't listened to her because she had gone through a couple of dozen men and got nothing for it but herpes and heart ache.

Yet, I lose no sleep over my son now. He is a successful accountant, husband, father of three and part-time basketball coach. Even though he didn't have a consistent father in his life, he had done well having had Elliott in his life during his formative years. He had seen the essence of real manhood firsthand. I raised him in the church and made sure he knew right from wrong. Mary instilled good values in him and taught him to respect other people. When Hassan was accepted to college with scholarships and grants to boot, I was beyond proud. I was beside myself because I knew that, from that point on, he would be able to take care of himself. Hassan was basically set for life at thirty-five, but our roles had reversed somewhat because I called on his help more often than I cared to remember. From now on, I decided, I would not keep bothering Hassan for help. He had a wife and his own children to raise. I never wanted to force him to say no to his mother because it would be all too painful for both of us. Plus, I needed to establish and maintain my own independence - if not for my own confidence, at least for the sake of self-respect.

When Hassan was about thirteen, we spent a lot of time with Keith Mackie, an old high school friend. Keith was a card-carrying black militant. He called me "Queen" and wanted to marry me but, although I was attracted to Keith, I could not take the chance on more heartbreak. Keith persisted, but the relationship remained platonic although he never gave up on Hassan or me as a single, black mother. Keith would tell me there was an unwritten plan to destroy the black family. He said, "Even during the civil rights era, there were more nuclear black families than there are now." He theorized that "the man" had taken jobs out of the community, diverted school funds to the suburbs, brought in drugs and allowed the black female to excel over the male, thereby emasculating the man. Back then, it all sounded a bit extreme to me, but looking at the occasional highs and consistent lows for the masses of blacks, I now feel Keith hadn't been too far off. Much of what Keith said back then resonates with me today.

I looked around the beautiful loft home I created for myself. I adored the high ceilings, exposed brick and huge wall sized industrial windows overlooking the Phoenix skyline. I plopped down on my down-wrapped, sectional couch in front of the 72" wide screen TV hanging over a contemporary, low-slung console and flipped through the channels. I landed on ESPN where the Pelicans were playing the Raptors and was happy to see my favorite player, "Boogie," ballin' and being appreciated. I've done well, all things considered, I thought. I have a fresh, modern place to live in, full of all my favorite things. I was able to raise my little boy into the successful young man he has become, even though I hadn't achieved what I set out to do originally. I can't think of a better result than being able to say I bore, loved and raised a black boy to manhood. That, in and of itself, is a monumental achievement in America. No, he didn't end up playing for the league as he'd hoped to, but he did become a responsible person, a professional and a family man, holding it together with strength and dignity.

That's been my focus and I achieved success, so now what? What am I going to do with the rest of my life? Find another gig and just keep cruising the malls, shopping at Marshall's, TJ Maxx or HomeGoods looking for sale items every weekend? Or maybe I could take up a hobby, re-decorate this place, or start going to the gym more often. Would I be content if I did that?

Now, in a solemn mood, I knew that I had run out of daydreams, errands and projects. I was officially procrastinating and needed to get down to business. I recalled my old idea of a modern day, "Back-to-Africa" program. I wondered to myself if an updated "Back-to-Africa" program was even a good idea period. Would folks even care? Would people think it was one of those Dimona-Black Hebrew Israelite-like communes? Who even knew if anyone even wanted to go back to Africa? Could I make a living running such a program? Conditions in Africa today, to many people, seem not much better than they were in the past, although it's not true. There are many positives on the continent of Africa and I knew that firsthand having traveled twice to West Africa in my lifetime. Somehow, in America, we never get to see the skyscrapers in Lagos or the high-end shopping and museums in Dakar. Even in the 1970's, there were modern cities and luxurious beachfront hotels along the shores of West Africa. We've been taught to think that everything about blacks or what we have is inferior, which is totally false. Listening to the radio in the background, I sang along with the lyrics of Lauren Hill's jam, *"Everything is Everything,"* which rang so true to my ears:

> "I wrote these words for everyone who struggles in their youth
> Who won't accept deception, instead of what is true?
> It seems we lose the game
> Before we even start to play
> Who made these rules?
> We're so confused

Easily led astray. Let me tell you that everything is everything…"

After the game, I grabbed a writing pad and watched the news while enjoying a cup of mint tea in a floral, vintage bone china cup and saucer. Shaking my head, I lamented the latest story of another unnecessary, fatal shooting of a black person. I wondered to myself if there would ever be a time when we would not be deluged with constant messaging of disdain and bias against blacks. Our psyches are forced to absorb this negativity nearly every day of our being in this country. I sighed and returned to my choices for a business. I want to do something that would bring about wholeness and dignity to Americans descended from Africa, but I didn't know what. On my days of low morale, I would say, "It's something God's got to do," but I knew that God also works through us recalling the fabled story of a sea stranded man who turned away boats and helicopters waiting for God to save him and God telling him, well I sent you help and you turned it away.

I looked at my pad and went over each program idea. Not wanting to move too fast, I considered the black history website idea which seemed narrow enough to actually work. The lessons would start in the period of earliest human civilization, which was found in Africa. It would continue to the times of Ancient Ethiopia and cover each Egyptian dynasty, then it would move forward in time and cover the middle ages, the period of "the great migration" of Africans. After that, it would break down the European slave trade, which happened much later in the larger scheme of things. After each lesson, there would be thoughtful testing, designed to evoke critical thinking, not rote regurgitation of facts. The only problem with the website idea was the challenge of offering the lessons free of charge.

I then turned to the "right of passage" program. It could take place over a week and would include topics from self-realization, to the basics of finances, nutrition and manners. My worry about that idea was whether today's black parents would embrace the need for such training. I felt it was vital because many of us aren't even raising our children these days. Too many are falling to addiction, bad choices and other ills resulting in many of our children winding up in the foster care system, graduating on to the juvenile delinquency system and from there to the "big house." They become adults without having any foundation or home training and we wonder why our progress is so slow. That's not to say that it's all our fault or even mostly our fault since discrimination and systemic racism tend to ensure bad results by design. But even though I saw it this way, I didn't know if other black parents would agree and embrace that kind of program.

I continued to look at other business ideas, but my mind kept wandering back to the Motherland. "Protests have broken out across all the major cities, towns and hamlets in America," said a reporter on the national news playing on the other widescreen television, this one above my fireplace. "People are protesting against the brutality, injustice and hatred black people have to bear each and every day." The reporter asked a protester holding a sign while marching with others on the street that said, #Black Lives Matter, "Excuse me Sir, why are you here?" He replied, "I just can't take it anymore."

Eventually, a resolve came over me and I made an executive decision about my life. The best way out may be to leave.

CHAPTER 4

Spirit

Once our families settled in and integrated with the other families, I decided to accept things as they were, giving up my silent protest against the move. I had secretly longed to return to Homer where life was predictable and slow. In this new land, there were hundreds more people around and I didn't know their names or understand their speech. Over time though, I learned their language and even learned how to write in their language, something we did not do before going to the place called Kemet.

Looking back, even after becoming an adult, how could I have known then that I was living during one of the periods of preeminent black glory, one of our heights of dominance, our African people having originated and produced scientific, engineering, architectural and intellectual achievements unknown to mankind at that time and still to this day the basis for most of the magnificent accomplishments of human civilization to this day? They developed quarrying, surveying and irrigation techniques. They founded novel and astonishing construction, mathematical and medical milestones. They produced innovative agricultural systems and advanced stonework. Considered one of the world's first writing system, hieroglyphs facilitated an unprecedented form of communication between Africans. Africans developed a calendaring system and clocks and lived by a defined system of government all those centuries ago. It was our time and we can forever be proud of our ancestors for our rich history and for the perseverance they demonstrated in good and bad times throughout the centuries.

The life span of any good thing though ends sooner or later. After my physical death, God Almighty allowed me to observe the changes in the land that become known as Egypt and I witnessed first-hand what happened to our people through the many dynasties of Ancient Egypt and beyond.

CHAPTER 5

Karima

Having settled on a business concept, I was relaxed enough to get back to my "come back" plan. I took a long look at myself in the mirror and sighed. My skin was even and fairly taut. I high fived my reflection in the mirror, relishing the fact that I had absolutely no sagging skin, not even above my neck. Although I preferred to get my self-esteem from within, my other side was beginning to long for male attention because it had been absent from my life for so many years. I removed the blunt cut wig and admitted to myself that the look was far less than authentic and far less attractive than my full, shoulder length, natural hair when it is styled. I decided to get a precision blunt cut that would fall just right whether flat ironed or natural and that I would get my huge, dark moles removed by a dermatologist. I also decided to figure out a strategy to lose thirty to thirty-five pounds and get down to a size ten again. I had already been looking at make-up tutorials on the Internet and learned how to contour and "beat my face" as they say in New York. The process should take about six months and be sustainable if I get regimented and don't fall back on bad habits and laziness.

Inwardly, I wondered if my anticipated new look would attract male attention. In many ways, I wanted it, craved it. Over the years, I had made celibacy and single life look easy but, in truth, it had been very difficult and lonely. I had even begun to think I was not meant for love and companionship. I hoped that wasn't true because I was beginning to really want a chance at romance. Hassan was set with a wife and children, so I couldn't use him as an excuse for staying alone anymore. My real fear was that I couldn't attract a suitor since I had let myself go. I laughed out loud when I thought about an older man who approached me in a restaurant telling me I was a very beautiful woman. Then, he reared back and studied me saying, "Yeah, you had your day!" Horrified, I had a mind to sock the nut, but all I could do was laugh at the weakness of his pick-up game. The incident was funny but telling at the same time since it was a reminder to me that I needed to pick up my own game! Anyway, I'll "have my day" again once my makeover is complete, I hoped.

I looked around my home and tidied up. Hassan had moved out before I bought the place. It was a listing I handled back in 2007 during the real estate crisis. I got the loft apartment for a steal and took my time decorating it in what I called "Moroccan-Scandinavian" design. I still have some traditional leanings though. For instance, every season, I decorate my ten-seat dining table with holiday themed place settings and decorations. I never considered myself creative or artsy, but decorating that table several times a year is something I enjoy immensely. God is so wonderful I thought, to give us such a variety of talents, gifts and personalities, all for his glory, but we get to enjoy them as well.

My loft is airy and colorful, painted differing shades of gray and yellow throughout. It is the perfect environment to inspire me to do what I can do to help somebody else through my ambitious business idea. Starting to make notes on my writing pad, I thought, this would not be Marcus Garvey's Back-to-Africa program of the early 1900's. No, it would be a return to the Motherland for the millennium. I figured going back to Africa, if nothing else, would be a reminder to us and to the world that we are not a lost people without a home. We came from somewhere and have someplace to go back to. If one feels that America is their home, they have a right to that by all accounts. But if one cannot accept their peculiar predicament in this country, they would have an option.

As I pondered the sheer magnitude of the project, I realized it would take big money to pull it off. I created a spreadsheet and started a proposed budget estimating costs for travel, land, new construction, officials, orientations, staffing, build outs, chaperones, hotels and housing. I estimated the base costs to exceed just over fifteen thousand dollars per person. I wondered to myself, who would pay for all this? Figuring God would work it out, I thought about the potential impact in Africa. The program policies must include a benefit to the hosting countries and to the African continent itself. That meant local jobs and industries would have to be created to make the plan sustainable.

There was also the issue of whether Africans would welcome their kindred brothers and sisters' home. Relations between Africans and American Blacks were not what some might expect. Ancient hurt and misunderstanding about how Africans allowed this to happen subconsciously plagues Blacks in America, especially when you are told, "they sold you." They don't see that it was a cunning defense asserted by the people who thought it was alright to own and enslave other human beings, whether paid for or not. On the other hand, Fatou told me that many Africans feel superior to American Blacks whom Africans ironically consider degenerate, mixed breeds and descendants of slaves. There are many Africans who do not want the "children of the diaspora" to come back and re-establish themselves in Africa, yet they welcome foreigners who they believe just want to help them! They should know they are there for the rich, natural resources and for the land itself. Whatever the perspective, there are healthy minded blacks on both sides who could make a modern day, well-conceived Back-to-Africa program work. Our people absolutely must learn from the past. I made plans to meet with Fatou as soon as possible and then I called Skanki to fill her in although I knew it might be a mistake.   21

"Girl, you done lost it! Back-to-Africa? Really?" I said, "Yeah, why not?" Sensing my discomfort with her negativity, Skanki brought it down a tad. "Alright Karima, you're making some good points but, personally, I'm not trying to be nobody's third wife or walk around barefoot." "Foolio, you need to educate yourself," I told her. "You done bought into every lie and stereotype there is about Africa. There may be some places where polygamy is practiced or where life is simple, but the opposite is also true," I told her emphatically. "Girl, I'm messing with you. I think it's a good idea actually and if I can get one of those fine 'brothas over *theeerrrre*, I'll join the program myself," said Skanky, and we both fell out laughing. After we hung up, I called Fatou before I allowed Skanki's nonsense to permeate my positive point of view.

CHAPTER 6

Fatou

"What's up Powers?," I said after seeing Karima's name on my caller ID. After the customary reports to each other on the health and welfare of our respective family members, Karima told me that she had something very exciting to tell me. Karima said, "Fatou, I got fired girl, and I believe it was a blessing because it's compelling me to chart my own course. I'm starting an enterprise that I would like for you and Kofi to be involved in as co-founders." "Do tell," I said. "Bottom line, it's a start-up, modern day, Back-to-Africa program." "Girl, you may have something with that since I know a lot of brothers and sisters are anxious to get up out of here because of everything going on right now." Karima responded, "Yep, people are already relocating to the Motherland without help, but I believe a structured program would ensure benefits to both the relocators and to the countries they settle in." She continued, "Since you guys are in Atlanta and this is my idea, I'd love to come for a visit and maybe bring my granddaughters with me and we can really hash it out in person." "Sounds great because the girls can visit some of the many HBCUs in the area for future reference while they're here," I replied. After discussing the idea further, we hung up and I reflected on the conversation.

For me, Karima was the metaphoric long lost, beloved sister. One taken and abducted by savages, but somehow restored to my arms. The friendship between us was deep and true. We had met at the local city college about thirty-five years ago. In our history class, I related to many of Karima's comments and observations. I invited her to join my study group and the rest was history.

I remember how Karima, with her pecan colored skin, warm, round eyes and dimples, had to beat the men off. She had natural charisma and seemed to be going somewhere in life given her keen intellect and passion for learning. I inwardly cringed when popular, no-count Malcolm Barnes started going after her. I peeped his game and intuitively knew his interest in her was fleeting at best. Ultimately, Karima was blessed with a son, but had to drop out of school and literally give up her life to raise him alone.

Thinking back to our many afro-centric type conversations back-in-the-day, Karima openly envied me for being born African and having an identifiable country of origin and told me so. Karima would say she felt cheated and confused by the predicament of blacks in America where, on the one hand, America is your country because you were born here and your family and known roots are here. On the other hand, racism and discrimination are constant reminders of our past enslavement and subjugated positioning in this country. Blacks in America, she would argue, are double minded, having to proclaim allegiance to a land where they experience unrelenting discrimination. A slippery slope indeed.

In one such conversation, Karima really dropped science on us. She unabashedly told our study group, comprised of mostly African students, that in her spirit, she knew that black people were very special and ruled the earth at one time. She schooled us on the magnificent achievements of Ancient Africans, later called Egyptians, but she wondered out loud what happened to us after that, having been so advanced and brilliant but winding up being plundered and allowing foreigners to remove over twelve million people off the continent. Visibly shaken and angry that day, adding that not only do American Blacks not know why fellow Africans could not prevent that from happening, she also wondered why American Blacks weren't even curious about what went wrong in Africa during those times for something so extreme and horrific to happen to us.

She said that American Blacks seem satisfied to learn so-called black history starting in 1619, when black slaves allegedly hit the shores of the Americas, as if that is the beginning of our story. She desperately wanted to know for herself and for other blacks to really know their true history, in its totality, lest it be repeated. Well, many years have passed since then and Karima made it her business to research and find out what happened between the times of Ancient Ethiopia, from about 3000 BC, and the European slave trade in around 1600 AD, and the information she gleaned helped her to find a kind of peace. On the day of that conversation many years ago, I made a mental note to never underestimate the depth of the feelings of American Blacks again and to keep Karima in my friendship forever. Coming back to the present, after much consideration, I decided it would be an honor to partner with Karima and bring the family of Africans back together. I just needed to get my husband on board.

I am from an established Ghanaian family which can be traced back hundreds of years. I work as the Nursing Administrator at a local hospital. I married Kofi Diallo, a pediatrician, thirty years ago. I met Kofi, also from Ghana, at Walton University where I transferred after two years of City College. Kofi had been a no-nonsense student. He proposed to me on our first date, but I slowed him down to make sure he was the right choice for me. He was. Five years later, we started our family and ultimately had three boys, Matthew, Karnwie and Luka, now adults. We both come from large families and we are all very close.

My Kofi, an Isaiah Washington look alike, is given to detail and initially dismissed the idea of co-founding a Back-to-Africa program, but he softened after pillow talk. He looked at our picture on the nightstand, palmed my chin, looked in my eyes and said in a pick-up artist voice, "I adore you my beautiful wife with your flawless mocha colored brown skin, high cheekbones, almond shaped eyes and a swan like neck, so I guess I'll keep you and give some thought to what you are talking about," he joked. "Seriously though, you are the very image of royalty my love," he added. I thanked him with a kiss.

We continued to talk about Karima's proposition and he acknowledged that, understandably, some American Blacks had no real sense of belonging in America given the bitter history and also because of their anger and frustration with present day events. "We know first-hand since we are black as well, but it seems less cogent for us as immigrants," he added. "Does Karima have financial backing," he asked? "Not that I know of Kofi, but where there is a will, there is a way," I responded. Kofi replied, "After thinking about it, Karima's plan might be just what we've been looking for to add purpose to our lives. God's plan for all of us will be fulfilled. Absolutely nothing happens without him causing it or by him allowing it to happen," Kofi said. He concluded that Karima's plan should be part of our future as well since we are uniquely able to help her bring it to fruition. Kofi told me that his gut told him that fate, also known as God's plan, was in play in the vision given to Karima.

CHAPTER 7

Spirit

After a while, it became obvious that the interlopers from across the Red Sea in Northwestern Asia were desirous of the lush, fertile lands of the region inhabited and developed by Africans. While they initially presented as traders and brothers, they soon wanted to set up settlements and eventually amassed a stronghold in our kingdoms in Lower Egypt. Eventually, there was no point in hiding their ambitions to covet our land and assume credit for our practices, inventions, intellectual systems, mathematics, spirituality, monuments, art and architecture from the time of the earliest dynasties of Ancient Egypt.

Thus, throughout early Egyptian history, wars between Africans against Asian interlopers for control over parts and the whole of North Africa took place. The "Asians" were a variety of peoples from the adjacent continent of Asia, from different countries and different religions. Our people, the Africans, were a peaceful people and were often unprepared to defend themselves against invaders with more potent and developed weaponry. Nevertheless, from afar, I personally saw Africans successfully drive foreigners from our land numerous times, while some African Kings favored policies of tolerance and assimilation. These contrasting viewpoints began to cause division and diminished trust amongst the Africans who had built one of the first highly developed civilizations on earth.

Karima's forefathers, who were of Nubian descent, were related to Memnon, a legendary Nubian king who fought in the Trojan War. The Nubians, African peoples, had impressed the Greeks for centuries to the point that they told stories of the Nubians calling them the "tallest and handsomest on earth." But even more impressive to the Greeks was their piety. The Greeks acknowledged in their own writings and oral history that the "Ethiopians," translated to mean the "burnt-faced ones," which is what the Greeks called the Nubians, were of such great piety and spirituality that the Gods "preferred their offerings over that of all other peoples." Even back then, we were known for our beauty and great capacity for hope, faith and love.

During the time of slavery in America, I came to know the workings of the "one drop rule" where any Black blood, even a mere drop, classified you as Black. On the contrary, in Ancient Egypt, the products of marriages between African women and men from other groups garnered people of mixed blood who identified with their father's lineage to the exclusion of the Africans. Yet, the women of the other peoples were off limits, never mixing with African men. It got so that the mixed blood offspring of the African women and the other men were devoted to the foreigners and that group had disdain for the Africans. My spirit ached viewing Africans becoming less and less united and I watched them grow to distrust each other, which was unheard of during my time on earth.

Still, throughout those thousands of years, many African kings were wise and strong and fought for our land and legacy. Other kings were not and lost ground in the fight to maintain our land and the truth of African history and magnificence. As we lost ground over time, the names of iconic African people, places and things were changed and the images of monuments and architectural structures were altered and superimposed to appear non-Black to erase the fact that Africans were the founders and architects of what became known as Egypt. My heart broke over and over again for my people as I bore witness to lies and injustice. Back then, even I could not have known that the future of our people would continue to be plagued by challenges and hardship for centuries upon centuries. Incredulously, that Egypt was even a part of Africa was later denied as foreigners captured the land. Its inhabitants went from dark skin tones to near white over hundreds of years. Over many centuries, foreigners overtook that region of Northern Africa and Africans were pushed south of Egypt and our role in the history of Northern Africa going back to the earliest dynasties was denied.

Blacks were eventually forced out of Egypt altogether by around mid-600 BC. After that, the Nubians began a great migration south of Egypt over many centuries where they were further frustrated by nature, climate change and territorial conflict, making it very difficult to re-establish themselves.

CHAPTER 8

But seek ye first the kingdom of God and his righteousness and all these things shall be added onto you. Matthew 6:30

Karima

I am more determined than ever to get moving on the program after speaking to Fatou. For one thing, Fatou told me that she and Kofi had access to funds, at least enough to get it going. With them on board, a weight was lifted off my shoulders since I would have some help handling the vast amount of details needed to kick off the effort. Once I get to Atlanta for that first meeting, we can come up with a name for the program and arrange for incorporation of the business. We can also work on creating a PowerPoint presentation to organize our thoughts and move things along. It was so interesting that each founding member, each of the three of us, brings a particular expertise to the table, so to speak. I am the visionary, historian and strategist. Fatou is the administrator and IT specialist by trade. Kofi, the legal and funding "go to" person.

Life had really changed for me in less than a week. I had gone from "all none void," to quote vintage rap lyrics, to "boss" status "makin' thangs happen". "Look at God," I said to myself. It suddenly occurred to me that my life had particularly evolved since I devoted myself to the Lord. I had grown so much spiritually since I began attending the "Covenant," my church home. The word was taught so clearly by our Pastor and was always backed up by scripture. I could not help but learn basic Christan principles, which for me

boiled down to loving God and other people, believing in Jesus and the resurrection and maturing spiritually. I had even learned to be a better steward of the money God put in my hands which is how I had finally amassed savings, however meager they were. Before that, I was living paycheck-to-paycheck and could not even figure out how to live on a budget. It was as though the proverbial cloud of ignorance had been lifted from
above my head.

A spurt of divine energy compelled me to wax my brows. Afterwards, I assessed my progress on the "come back" program. I had lost eighteen pounds, had the moles removed courtesy of Dr. Kwame and got the haircut. I was using an airbrush tool to apply my foundation and utilizing the make-up techniques I learned online to give me a polished, but natural look. My grandchildren, Marie, Madeline and Lois, watched me over a few weeks transform from my standard look to something much better. This new routine was so different, I wondered if I had gone too far, but they assured me that I was on point and gave me a new nickname, "Glammie." My granddaughters egged me on and told me I had become a "baddie" and a "straight playa."

The trip to Atlanta came and went. The girls toured a few historically black colleges including Spelman and Clark Atlanta University, escorted by Fatou's sons, considered their "cousins." They enjoyed lunch at a celebrity owned restaurant and spotted a few "stars," so that was the highlight of the trip for them. Meanwhile, the adults focused on the job at hand and completed a dynamic PowerPoint presentation for potential investors. Fatou channeled her administrator persona and ran the meeting. After she tolerated a spell of reminiscing and clowning, she called the meeting to order. "We are going to work backwards with our timeline," she said, and asked me when I aspired to launch the project. I responded, "I figure one year tops." Kofi replied, "That may be a bit overly ambitious since marketing, funding, publicity and land purchases are all open projects. It may take a year just to get those things in place, let alone be operational." Gently biting my lip, I agreed that more than a year may be needed, but stressed that much could be accomplished by the twelve-month mark if everything goes our way.

As a group, we agreed on a name for the program, "Motherland Bound." We used a service to incorporate right then and there using my debit card. I was proud to be able to pull out my card and charge over three hundred dollars without worrying with trembling fingers. I had come a long way and my friends knew it as they beamed with pride for my newfound financial determination. In my mind, I wondered to myself if my friends would have been willing to go down this road with the old, broke Karima and was thankful I was past all that now. Describing himself as the CFO, to our amusement, Kofi informed us that he would arrange a future meeting with an attorney friend, who also had accounting credentials, to set up the not-for-profit to meet legal standards regarding taxes and structure. Kofi's medical office had a "for-profit" legal composition, so he did not know the ins and outs of non-profit structure.

We discussed the need to have an office to work from and decided to rent a modest space in Phoenix for me. Kofi pledged fifty thousand dollars from his foundation for start-up capital and promised to open the corporate account the following week. That way, the office space could be rented and the funds would also be sufficient to pay weekly salaries to us, the founder/consultants, as well as fund an office assistant pending future deposits from contributors. I hated to take money from the budget but admitted to myself that I really did need a salary to pay my bills and maintain some savings for cushion. Kofi and Fatou did not tell me until later that they did not actually want consulting actually want consulting fees, but they insisted we all be paid to ensure I earned a salary. Moved deeply by the large contribution from Kofi's foundation and by the way they both embraced my idea, I thanked them profusely. I broke down and cried tears of joy. We ended the meeting with a prayer asking for the blessing of the Lord on our new business and upon our families.

CHAPTER 9

"They said to each other, "Come, let's make bricks and bake them thoroughly. They used brick instead of stone, and tar for mortar. Then they said, "Come, let us build ourselves a city, with a tower that reaches to the heavens so that we may make a name for ourselves; otherwise we will be scattered over the face of the whole earth.

But the Lord came down to see the city and the tower the people were building. The Lord said, "if as one people speaking the same language they have begun to do this, then nothing they plan to do will be impossible for them. Come, let us go down and confuse their language so they will not understand each other." So the Lord scattered them all over the earth, and they stopped building the city."

-Genesis 11:3-8

Spirit

Usually, I'm in and out of consciousness but, as God would have it, I followed Karima's life from the very beginning. I really believe God allowed me to have consciousness during Karima's lifetime because she was the one he designated to unite the children of the diaspora through her thoughtful program. If I could, I would tell the children the story of their ancestors and answer Karima's question about what was going on in Africa that was so extreme that we could not prevent the taking of millions of countrymen and women off the continent. But there's only so much I can do in my present state.

As the Nubians were pushed south of Egypt, under terrible conditions, they migrated throughout Africa, often on the run from foreign slave mongers. They also ran from each other, as groups formed and fought each other for limited habitable land. Many of these groups continued to migrate even further south of the Sudan, for hundreds and hundreds of years, in search of fertile soil, water and life supporting conditions, to the exclusion and sometimes the detriment of each other. Ultimately, before meeting other independent tribes already living in Central and Southern regions of Africa, like the Khoisan, the Bantu and the Great Zimbabweans, these groups formed, in the interim, thousands of tribes, languages and cultures, often in a vacuum. Karima wondered how we winded up speaking so many different languages and dialects in Africa, and this is one explanation for how it happened.

Even once a settlement of people was established, housing was not always able to be built for the long term as the migrating population looked for land on which they could re-establish farms. Instead, housing was often built to be left on a moment's notice, hence, "hut" housing as opposed to the palaces and more permanent residences of their Egyptian past. Some scholars have described this period of assaults against the Nubians and the surrounding kingdoms as the First World War which went unreported and ignored in world history. So, while some African peoples were in a state of dis-ease where starvation and chaos persisted for centuries at a time, other groups did eventually come together with other Africans south of the Sahara forming the foundation for cities and countries of the future. Existing kingdoms in Mali, Ghana and other places sustained themselves for centuries, but foreign opposition to African independence in their own land was strong and the kingdoms did not last.

This was the condition of our people when Europeans joined the exploitation of Africans making slave mongering, death and destruction easy against a fractured, disunited and beleaguered people scattered about, speaking hundreds of dialects and languages. To be blunt, our people were in no condition to defend themselves by the time European slave mongers entered into the picture. We were isolated from each other, spoke more than two thousand different languages and dialects and did not trust each other. We were easy pickings for the slave "trade."

CHAPTER 10

Karima

As the founder, I was tasked with finding suitable board members. By law, five members was a sufficient number of people to form a non-profit board of directors and Fatou, Kofi and I could legally be included as members. I set out to find two more members. I chose Darius Jones, a frat brother of Kofi I had met years ago, who also happened to live in Phoenix. Darius was smart, good looking and conscious. I had not seen him in a few years, but trusted that he had not changed much. I selected Simone Davies as the final member. Simone had been the school principal when Hassan was in high school and we had formed a solid friendship during those years. Simone was retired and had time to become involved. She had recently told me that she was becoming bored in retirement even with all the reading she did. A scholar of black history, Simone was working on black history software to pitch to library systems nationwide. I knew Simone would be perfect for the board since she was level-headed and was always bent towards conciliation. Board members wield a lot of power, particularly for non-profits, and we founders wanted to avoid potential power struggles interfering with our mission.

Even though everything was clicking and moving forward, I found myself feeling uneasy and panicky at times. Those emotions were beginning to take over. I decided to write down my feelings to try and get to the bottom of my fears and then go to God in prayer to overcome them. Preferring paper and pen to typing, I wrote out my concerns and then read over my notes about how I was feeling. The notes revealed a number of fears such as flying frequently, the uncertainty of the outcome, the massive amount of money needed to manage the program and finally, fear of failure. I immediately got down on my knees and spoke to the Lord. I asked for forgiveness for fear and doubt and I asked for strength and a sound mind to see it through. I asked the Lord for traveling mercy and abatement of fear itself, which is not of God. I asked it all in the name of Jesus and I fell into a peaceful sleep.

The next morning, I got up, dressed and headed to the office, which had been secured in the arts district downtown to save costs. I fell out laughing when I noticed just how much I had changed. Number one, being late was not even an issue since I was in charge. It was funny because I couldn't wait to get there and had totally overcome piddling around in the morning causing chronic tardiness. The other thing, of course, was my look. It amazed me how enjoyable shopping, dressing and grooming had become. Every evening, I seriously ponder what to wear the next day and carefully choose jewelry and accessories to coordinate my look. All my life, deep down, I had wanted to keep up my physical appearance, but either lacked the time, money or motivation to get it done. Somewhere along the way, I found my inspiration. The more frequent "cat calls" probably hadn't hurt either. I was actually enjoying positive attention and I felt so good about myself. Somewhere in heaven, Mary and Elliott were doing flips of joy.

Not long after I got into the office, board member, Darius Jones, walked in. I gave him a warm welcome, but felt somewhat uncomfortable with him being there for no particular reason. It was the second time I had seen him since he accepted the Board position. He told me he was there to get another copy of the marketing plan before the upcoming meeting. He said, "Karima, you look lovely in yellow," and I blushed. After getting the copy, Darius uncharacteristically hugged me. Taken aback, I returned the hug, but it was awkward. A notorious "Kappa," Darius was a "tall drink of water" with his warm brown eyes and a toned physique, but his showing up like that still rattled me. It wasn't fear *per se* since Darius was a friend of Kofi's and a recognized community leader, but I still did not feel comfortable around him for some reason. It might have been the way he was undressing me with his eyes.

At the board meeting a week later, Darius made a motion that had everyone scratching their heads. He moved that we reconsider the program name, "Motherland Bound," because he said it was not catchy enough. He suggested another name, "Destination Africa." He also told the group "the program was flawed since it should be expanded to include others besides the "children of the diaspora." His comments garnered a collective gasp and were unceremoniously shot down. During the discussion phase, Kofi questioned Darius about his "inclusiveness" proposition and he merely said it was the right thing to do. His sudden change of perspective was duly noted. After all, world citizens from all over the continent can choose to relocate to another country, subject to immigration laws, without a reason or agency behind them. This program, however, was intended to address a particular demographic, for a particular reason. We all began to consider that Darius may have changed.

Still, we pressed on with our plans. Unanimously, we decided to travel to West Africa to present the program to local community leaders and politicians in Senegal, Liberia and Ghana. Both Kofi and Fatou had significant contacts in West Africa and could set up meetings with counterparts of power and influence. In many ways, securing land and partnerships in Africa was the main priority because without them, there was nothing to promote or plan. I was beside myself with excitement for the trip scheduled to take place in thirty days. No one was disappointed when Darius told us he would not be able to make the trip. He really had me feeling some kind of way with his flirting on the one hand, but being contrary on the other. I was disappointed that Simone would miss it as well, but she promised to go on the next opportunity.

Feeling hopeful, I decided to use a few dollars from my savings to shop for the trip. Having lost weight, I needed clothes anyway I reasoned with a naughty grin on my face.

CHAPTER 11

Kofi

Karima doesn't know what Darius is up to, but I do. Darius is one of those confused brothers who have a love/hate relationship with other blacks. During his college years, he embraced his culture, attending an HBCU and joining a fraternity. He dated, played ball and enjoyed the popularity that came with his profile. After graduating however, his leanings became more conservative after climbing the ladder at a public utility. The higher his salary went, the more distance he put between himself and his culture. In the community, he played the role of a black male role model, but his politics were conservative.

I realize now that Karima didn't know that Darius wasn't the same person we had known back-in-the-day, but I didn't want to cast aspersions on her choice for a board member who she met through me. Now, I regret not speaking up.

I decided to give it more time hoping Darius will come around. He had been a genuine, solid person at one time I reasoned. During the board meeting, I noticed how much Darius blatantly stared at Karima even though he is very married to an Italian woman he said he met through work.

CHAPTER 12

Darius

"What a waste of time," I thought to myself as I walked into my well-furnished and bedecked home office and man cave. The "cave" included a bar fully stocked with spirits and was accessorized with barstools, a glassed-in wine collection, cigar humidor and the room opened out onto a side yard with a mini putting green and bocce ball court. Didn't they realize their mission was hopeless? I'm not sure why I allowed myself to get involved with this mess, I thought. But, deep down, I knew why. I've had a thing for Karima since I met her all those years ago but couldn't get next to her because of her "no dating" policy after she became a young mother. If I'm honest with myself though, I was turned off that she went out like that. She was so young and cute back then, even after having a baby. But carrying on in such a stereotypical, black female fashion by getting knocked up and dropping out of school, I recognized that she wasn't on my level. But seeing how fine she still is after all these years, I still want her. I laughed to myself, "being a married man never stopped me before."

Thinking about the meeting again, I opened the French door across from my deck and walked outside to sit at the lawn table. I jotted down some thoughts in my "notebook." They had essentially debased me in the meeting for proposing inclusiveness and I'm not going to be treated like that, not even by an old buddy. They might all be doing fairly well, but they don't know I'm pulling a half million a year and have the lifestyle of "P Diddy." "Betta ask somebody," I grunted.

I took my cell out of my pocket and called an attorney friend of mine and left a message. I need to get some clarity on some legal issues. Since the Board is composed of an odd number of people, to get my way on things, I will have to have two other like-minded board members. I need to take control because I know that the last thing African Americans need is to get caught up in outwardly rejecting the "land of the brave." I have to find a way to divert this so-called program of theirs to something more resembling one of those high end, socially conscious, "let's appreciate the third world cultures that colonialists have almost bled dry" travel opportunities which will be available to any race, creed or color, rather than a straight up Back-to-Africa movement. That's why I distance myself from hood rats, they are always feeling sorry for themselves and don't do enough to pull themselves up from the gutter. I have got to put a stop to this nonsense.

I laid back on my designer chaise lounge in my home office and envisioned Karima in my bed and thought about a few of the things I could do to her and what I would have her do to me. I acknowledged my own physical virtues in my mind and figured she was also attracted to me. I reminisced on how big her dimples were when she smiled at me. She wanted me. Just thinking about it made my heart flutter. Once they return from Africa, I will make my move. By the time I put it on her, she won't want to leave my side.

"Hey Honey, watcha' doin'? What are you thinking about?" Shocked, I hadn't heard my wife walk on to the patio. I jumped up out the chair and tried to avoid facing her frontally. Thank goodness I have on my 'tighty whities," I thought. Otherwise I would have had some 'splainin' to do.

CHAPTER 13

Karima

Brimming with pride and excitement, I called Hassan to set up a family meeting to take place before I left for the Motherland. They agreed to meet me at a nearby restaurant the next day and the whole family would come, at my request. Arriving early, I sat in the center of a beautifully set rectangular table on the outdoor terrace of the tastefully decorated restaurant with exposed brick walls, hanging plants and a magnificent fireplace in the center. It was the perfect setting for my congratulatory send off. I watched my son, his wife and kids trailing, walk in and weave through the other guest tables towards me. I thought, how beautiful, regal they all are - how fortunate I truly am, despite all that's happened these last four hundred years, I was able to produce this. My spell broke as the youngest ran past the rest of the family and jumped into my arms. "Hi Glammie!" she yelled, making other restaurant guests turn around and smile. The rest of the family took their seats and we proceeded to enjoy a delicious three course Italian meal.

As we conversed easily, Lois, my eleven-year-old granddaughter, said, "Glammie, why in the world would you think anyone wants to go back to Africa where everyone is starving or has Ebola?" Though annoyed, I had to laugh at the ludicrous question. Lois was the most precocious of my granddaughters. She was also a great student and always spoke her mind. I replied, "Because you shouldn't believe everything you hear." Lois and the girls had been raised in a non-diverse area of town where the good schools were located so they didn't have a lot of exposure to diverse opinions and perspectives. I tried to impart knowledge and wisdom when and where I could, hoping one day they would become critical thinkers and make a difference. I added, "Africa is the cradle of civilization. It is only natural to want ties to your ancestral homeland." Marie, fourteen years old and my oldest granddaughter, was smart and well read, more "woke" than the other two and was a gifted artist. She was excited for the possibilities and told her sisters about the "Nollywood" films she watched which had taught her a lot about modern Africa. Still, she added that she was "salty about them selling us." Madeline, a thirteen year old fashionista, smart and wise for her age, replied, "Well, even if they sold us, what can you say about people who bought, destroyed and enslaved other people for their own personal gain and yet, we were the ones they called savages." I complimented them on their insightful comments. I reminded them that it is important to read and study history in order to learn the truth. I told them that while some African chiefs and kings may have sold or traded other Africans for money, that practice was short lived and people were predominantly removed by brute, violent force. I decided that once I returned from my trip, I would give all of them some more reading to do. I made a mental note to ask Simone about the status of her black history website which I hoped recited history long before 1619.

Hassan knew I would take my safety seriously in Africa and just asked that I bring him something back. His wife, Ava, wanted to know when I would return. I gave them the date and described the itinerary. We finished our dessert and called it a night. I regretted I would miss Madeline and Lois' upcoming basketball game the next day. Having all of them in my life filled it with activity and excitement despite that I was a family of one. I was an absolute nut at the basketball games cheerleading for the girls. I would miss them while I was gone.

The next morning, I researched the weather for all three countries and learned it would be warm and humid while I was there. I bought linen, rayon and heat friendly outfits that were business casual and classy looking. I wanted to look every bit the executive I wanted to be. You gotta "fake it 'till you make it," I thought. Three months into my image transformation project, men were consistently giving me looks of interest, and women were studying my makeup, hair and outfits when I walked by. None of them actually approached me though. There was no more denying that I wanted a man in my life, but I would continue to wait on the Lord for the right one. Against my better judgment, I had been thinking about Darius and a little crush was developing in my heart. Luckily, before it took hold, Fatou mentioned his wife and daughter and the crush was dead on arrival. In my rational mind, I was relieved since getting involved with a board member was a bad idea, but I was still a little disappointed. I was beginning to hope that the Lord would send me someone soon because my mind and body were rebelling against me for the imposed sentence of decades of celibacy.

PART TWO

Back To Africa

CHAPTER 14

Karima

The next day, Fatou, Kofi and I headed to the airport from different cities for our respective flights to JFK. From there, we would fly to Dakar, Senegal, just across "the pond" known as the Atlantic Ocean. After four days in Senegal, we would drive to Monrovia, Liberia, which had been a destination of freed slaves in the mid-19th century. In fact, Monrovia was named in honor of US President James Monroe. My guess is that they did it because he had been "gracious" enough to let some of us go home. After four days in Liberia, we would fly to Accra, Ghana and stay there for one week.

All flights were without incident thankfully. I disembarked from the plane on the tarmac and broke down in tears when I saw the iconic Baobab tree of the African plain at the other end of the runway. Neither Kofi nor Fatou knew for sure why I cried, but they had an idea. For me, the pain of our history and the grief for what might have been was real. This time though, I was there to be a part of the healing process and to herald in the new renaissance. That thought brought a smile to my face to the relief of my traveling companions. Our program would not be for everyone, but for those who had a hole in their heart because of a sense of loss and displacement, this program could be their salvation. I reminded myself that our true worth is more than our plight in this world, as we are children of the "Most High" and no one can take that from you, ever. As bizarre as it may seem, God has allowed every bit of our history as a people and only he knows how it fits into his ultimate plan of redemption.

On this my third trip to West Africa, I was still overwhelmed with emotion. I took it all in. The local pediatrics association had provided an SUV and a handsome, professional driver by the name of Natu Bello for the entire trip. Natu reminded me of an African king with his sharp features and confident disposition. Once we settled into the drive, we enjoyed the landscape of "the bush" during the two hour drive across Senegal to a village called "Nafre," not far from Gambia, a bordering country. Nafre was near a beach resort called "Victoria's," where we would stay for three nights before moving on to Liberia.

During the ride, we passed many small villages and dwellings, which reminded me of one of the great ironies of the great migration of Africans centuries before. I commented that, "Africans erected simple housing structures which became known as "huts" which could be abandoned on a moment's notice if need be due to the predicament they were in hundreds of years ago. Fatou responded saying, "Yet, the hut model seems to have stuck in rural areas, probably due to its simple design and readily available building materials." Kofi agreed saying, "The continent literally lost millions of its youngest and strongest people and, not only were the lost people adversely affected, but Africa itself became terribly weakened by the fateful turn of events and the aftermath of colonialism on the continent."

Natu, a native Senegalese, had listened to the conversation silently up to that point. After Kofi's comment though, he spoke stating, "At one point, we believed we were all cursed. Our historical artifacts proving who and what we were, were stolen off our land and taken to European museums and other places. Thankfully, because our ancestors left so much evidence that could not be removed, it could not be credibly denied that Ancient Africans were profoundly brilliant and forward thinking. Yet, even still, we were told we had no history in our own homeland! Our ancestors fought time and time again to regain their land, sometimes triumphantly, sometimes not. Many of our people were taken away and those remaining were subjected to colonialism for a period. But, like our ancestors, we resisted and fought toppling colonialism in the mid-20th century. We are still re-building if you will, but "my hand was made strong by the hand of the Almighty," to quote soldier Bob Marley, and Africa will gain its rightful place in the world as God has planned." Spontaneously, Fatou, Kofi and I broke out in cries of jubilation. With that, Natu played Bob Marley's "Redemption Song" to the great pleasure of his riders. After we settled down, I noticed Natu staring at me through his rear view mirror. Soon, we pulled onto a long paved road lined with flowering hedges and trees. As we progressed, the trees became more sparse and the ocean was visible in the distance. We had arrived at one of the most beautiful beach vistas I had ever seen. The white stucco walls of the resort appeared as we continued down the road, which was actually taking on the orange, red and lavender glow of the sunset.

We checked into Victoria's and agreed to meet for dinner in two hours. I looked around my small but well-appointed room. It had a Caribbean vibe with turquoise colored walls and bamboo furniture, but the fabrics and textures were bright, geometric and ornate, authentically African. Our love of color and ability to spin shapes into the most eye-catching patterns isn't just Caribbean, Brazilian, or American, it comes from the Motherland, I remarked almost out loud to myself. This feels like home I thought. My previous trips to Africa with former church members had given me the same feelings. On those trips, I had enjoyed wider Accra and Dakar and I took time to reminisce. After a while, I unpacked and decided to try for a power nap. The potently masculine Natu popped into my head a time or two as I tried to find slumber.

Sleep would not come easy though as I was so pumped with adrenaline by it all. Just the thought that Africa's lost children could return and support the countrymen to further develop the homeland was so much to process. Excited about all the possibilities and the tasks that lay ahead, I looked for something to read - maybe a book or an article would calm my racing thoughts. I rummaged through the magazines and books I brought with me including Essence, Vogue, In Style and House Beautiful. Losing interest in all of them, I went through my suitcases and found my Bible in the outside pocket of one of the bags. As I flipped through it, searching for my last study section, I found a page bent to Romans. Reading out loud, I repeated the verse, "All things work together for the good of those who love God and who are called according to his purpose." (Romans 8:25. Meditating on that thought, I fell asleep comforted by the luxurious, gorgeous and soft bed linens.

I woke up to my cell phone buzzing on the pillow next to me. There was a text from Fatou to meet downstairs in twenty minutes for cocktails and dinner. I got it together and we were driven to a simply decorated restaurant and ordered our meals. The restaurant had no name and smelled of clean, unsoiled earth. We toasted the first night enjoying wine and a juice made from grapes produced by a vineyard in the area to the soft sounds of a local artist. Kofi blessed the food. We discussed the upcoming meeting with the Village Elders the next day. There were five hundred acres available for a long-term lease or sale, but we would need to convince the Elders that our plan was not one of exploitation, but one of mutual benefit. Kofi ordered a bottle of champagne and told us he had an announcement which would be a surprise. Candlelight highlighting her flawless brown skin, Fatou looked at him with feigned suspicion and raised an eyebrow. She was not accustomed to Kofi keeping secrets from her. Kofi looked back at his wife, his eyes twinkling with pride, then stood up and raised his stemware and said in a low tone, "We received a matching grant of five hundred thousand dollars from Lesson, Corp!" I fell back nearly out of my chair, and

Fatou shrieked with joy. Everyone in the restaurant looked in our direction with curiosity. "Foreigners," they probably thought. "Hold on, hold on," Kofi said, shouting over our hooping and hollering while trying to calm us down. "There is a contingency. First, we must raise the first $500,000, then we get their $500,000. Secondly, we have to build a new home community of one hundred small homes with the funds and create an upstart business that can produce seventy-five jobs and we have to do it all within eighteen months."

Beaming with pride, Kofi sat down to receive his props. Fatou and I hit him with a barrage of questions, mixed with praises to the Lord. Kofi explained that we needed to disclose the grant to the Elders and assure them that village residents, as well as relocating African Americans, would get those jobs and homes equally. Fatou said, "We should not have any push back on that since there is not a lot of industry in this area and everyone needs steady income." We discussed the need to have an experienced site manager and labor in place as soon as funds became available to meet the deadline. Kofi reminded us that we must all respect that approval of the Elders was not guaranteed as each village is sovereign and controlled by the Chief. Knowledge of local customs and decorum would be critical to our success. Based upon his upbringing in West Africa, Kofi told us that he would handle most of the presentation as men were expected to play leadership roles for the most part. Reluctantly, after much dispute, disagreement and debate, Fatou and I agreed to allow Kofi to lead the initial presentation. I fought back my resentment that a man was needed to present my idea although I knew Kofi would never upstage my role as the visionary.

Toasting and eating, we enjoyed a delicious meal of roasted chicken in a bed of field greens. After eating, we danced a while and retired early. I led the evening prayer before we separated and walked to our respective rooms. On my balcony alone now, I looked up at the night sky, lit with stars and a crescent moon that placed an iridescent glow on my skin. As I closed my eyes in a prayer of thanks. I felt someone or something looking at me. I shook it off and went inside my room for the night.

Natu

Natu gazed at Karima on her balcony from afar. She looked so beautiful and serene. His attraction to Karima was strong, actually pulling at his heart. Should he make his interest known he wondered? It might be the exact wrong thing to do as they all tried to be professional and handle program business. He decided to bide his time and see what unfolded.

CHAPTER 15

Karima

That next morning, we got into our car and Natu drove us to the meeting. I had to shake off the butterflies I felt fluttering in my stomach as I laid eyes on Natu again and willed myself to stay focused. We walked into a fading yellow stucco structure called the "Warma Building," and were led to a large room. The village itself consisted of small stucco homes in various dulled, pastel colors on the outskirts and larger buildings of the same colors in the village center. This part of Senegal was very green with an abundance of natural flowers, bushes and trees, not by human design, but by nature. The conference room was painted in a pale green color. Posters of events and prominent Africans lined the walls, including Kwame Nkrumah, the Obamas, Jerry Rawlings, Malcolm X, Dr. King and Nelson Mandela. There were four rectangular tables that were placed together forming a "T" shape. The meeting was set for 10:00 a.m. and we were early. To our surprise, adults of all ages and genders came in and greeted each other. It was obvious they all knew each other well. They laughed and talked with familiarity and genuine ease. One by one they came over and greeted each of us.

The meeting was called to order and each "Elder" pulled out their laptops and tablets and kept their cell phones nearby. I chucked to myself and thought, "so much for the Third World." They pulled up their agendas and Chief Anuna, a sixtyish, bald man, spoke first. He welcomed us and said they were honored to have been chosen for such an important collaboration,

"We are all Africans and we should come together to reclaim our legacy of greatness and resilience. Let us begin with an opening prayer to our Lord, Jesus Christ." They were Christians! After the prayer, Elder Bunmi Whey, a beautiful middle-aged woman, asked me to tell them about the proposal. Surprised to be asked to speak first for my group, I told them about my lifetime of wonder as to how our people could be taken from Africa and dispersed elsewhere. I told them that even before I found out the whys and the hows in response to my questions, I had envisioned a modern day Back-to-Africa program. I added that God created an opportunity for me to start a business having found able support from friends Fatou and Kofi. They all laughed when I admitted "the opportunity" was due to me being fired from a job. I went on to tell them the specifics of my vision. Later, Kofi laid out the terms and details of the matching grant. The Elders were visibly moved and impressed by all they heard except for Elder Tamu, a distinguished looking older gentleman who walked with a cane.

Elder Tamu was the oldest and the most stoic of the group of elders. He reminded the other Elders to slow down since they had certain questions that had yet to be answered and he proceeded with the first one. He questioned whether the agreements would be reduced to written contracts and, if so, who would be responsible for drafting. He also wanted to know if the background of those relocating would be investigated as he knew that many poor, American Blacks were prone to criminal behavior and might bring their habits to the Village. Fatou addressed Elder Tamu saying that it is rarely the individual's character that leads them to make bad choices, rather their circumstances. She said that anyone wanting to relocate to Africa would be doing so to get a new start, to do better, leaving a place where they felt they lost before they started the race. Elder Tamu seemed to relax after Fatou's last statement that rejecting people based upon their past would seem to be the ultimate rejection and act of cruelty absent extreme circumstances. He replied that he liked her way of thinking and that she had made a good point. He added that her concern for the plight of our people was very influential. Elder Tamu let it go after that. After more discussion, the project was approved pending contracts. We agreed to meet the next day for the formal presentations regarding industry and housing.

Natu, the driver, joined us for dinner that evening much to my pleasure. I had found myself thinking about him last night. Although Natu wasn't a member of the team, we had spent time with him and felt comfortable including him in the discussions. He had told us during the long drive that he was a carpenter by trade, so we knew he was bound to have valuable insight to impart on the next phase of the project, so we filled him in on what happened at the meeting. He, in turn, schooled us on construction norms in Senegal. We had all given forethought to potential industry and were more than ready to talk. I said, "I plan to make a presentation on developing a solar power plant, but I also think it would not hurt to start two areas of entrepreneurial pursuit. I couldn't help but be impressed by the grape juice we tasted last night, especially because the grapes were locally grown, bottled and distributed here, albeit on a very small scale." Fatou replied, "Karima, I am impressed. My idea was wind energy and bottled water, but I like your ideas better for this area given the regular direct sunlight and since the people already know how to farm the vineyards. We could export the juice internationally and sell energy to other towns and cities from our solar plant." Natu assured us that there was interest in the juice since restaurants in Dakar buy it regularly as well as wine from those same grapes.

Concerned about selling alcohol, I smiled at Natu and said, "I know that wine is probably more profitable, but if we bottle and sell it on a huge scale, that may encourage winos in not only Nafre, but in Senegal as well. Just saying that I would rather keep it clean and avoid potential addiction problems stemming from our program." Natu responded, "I never thought about that Karima and I definitely see your point." Kofi and Fatou nodded in agreement. "In black neighborhoods across America, there are liquor stores on practically every corner and it's not the same in other neighborhoods, so guess where alcohol addiction is more prevalent?" Fatou asked sarcastically. "As nouveau chic as a winery sounds, it comes with potential consequences for the very population we are trying to build up to whole mindedness. I agree we should nix wine production," Kofi concluded.

Kofi continued, "I had some ideas for commerce, but I will save them for Liberia or Ghana. For instance, Liberia has vast forestland from which rubber is derived from trees and plants. The timber there could be developed further and sustain lumber mills which could be the foundation for lumber manufacturing. We could also employ people in Liberia to plant, harvest, cut, clean and sell timber. We could use the products to build the homes for the relocators and local Africans so that they could live in close proximity and bring our people back together as one." Fatou gave Kofi a fist bump and said, "My man! Brilliant!" She added, "I might not be as creative and smart as the three of you, but I do watch television. All this reminds me of all the tiny home shows where people scale down their lives and live in homes as small as one hundred square feet in order to save money. The homes are mobile and allow their owners to move with ease. They are then free from hated jobs and the high costs of living so they become truly liberated, much more so than people with big houses and big mortgages. I'm not advocating that we build tiny homes, *per se*, but we could do a play on that idea and design prefab modest, but beautiful, functional floor plans based on simple design. If we used timber from Liberia or nearby locations, we could approve just a few home designs and have the wood precut for simplicity. If it is done right, the homes could be put up in weeks, not months," Fatou concluded. I shrieked and gave Fatou a big hug. I said, "Fatou, you nailed it, no pun intended." We all laughed with gusto.

Natu said, "Guys, I know I'm just the driver right now and I really appreciate you all even including me for dinner and in your discussion. I have to be honest though and tell you that I would love to be a part of what you are doing. As an experienced carpenter, I have built many homes and some from the ground up. In fact, I have three designs I could show you. Also, one I'm working on has a pyramid shaped design to honor the classic rural "hut" home type we talked about earlier. You can't let other people tell you the value of your revered icons. When you honor your culture and traditions, attitudes change fast."

"Natu, I believe the ladies will agree with me when I say that you are IN. Consider yourself a member of our team. It is amazing how all of our talents, contributions and ideas are in sync and come together like a puzzle, like it was meant to be. And you, my brother, have addressed a cornerstone need which makes me know Jesus is in this," Kofi said. We enjoyed the moment knowing that what was happening was right. As we finished our meal of incredible peanut butter based beef stew, we created an outline to present to the Elders in the morning. We prayed for mutual benefit regarding the decisions that would be made the next day and thanked the Lord for putting an experienced, Christian carpenter in our path. I silently thanked him for sending a fine one at that.

We all met the next morning in the same room in the Warma Building. Not having experienced much population growth in recent years, Elder Batu explained that they had not built homes in Nafre for some time, so they would listen to any suggestions on the topic. Since housing was the lighter topic, we decided to tackle it first. After the opening prayer, we started. Natu told the group more about his building experience and his credentials. He put his three-dimensional presentation on the big screen and broke down each proposed home model and the costs associated with each design. He told them they could adopt the "tongue and groove" method for ease of construction since all wood pieces would be cut to fit like puzzle pieces and would not require many tools for the most part. Kofi chimed in and explained his idea about getting lumber locally, including from other nearby countries, to not only support construction, but also to create jobs. Developing local lumber mills could create numerous jobs with many sub-specialties such as trimmers and cutters. We only had eighteen months to build one hundred homes although we hoped to get it done in less than a year. With the combination of local lumber, local labor and simple design, Natu said each home could be built for about ten thousand US dollars, not much in the grander scheme of things. Natu added that, "If costs can be met below that number, we will do so."

Chief Anuna moved to approve Natu's designs for one, two and three bedroom homes, which passed unanimously. I think the Elders felt even more comfortable with our program having a Senegalese man directly involved. Natu committed himself to incorporate some "off the grid" design features including solar panels and water saving plumbing devices. After a spirited discussion, the Team unanimously adopted the solar energy idea for industry development as well as the idea to expand the local grape vineyards. Kofi hoped out loud that the world was ready for grape juice from West Africa and everyone laughed heartily. The next meeting was set for ninety days out by conference call. By then, we expected funding to be in place so that we could commence the implementation phase of the program, both industry and housing.

CHAPTER 16

Karima

After we checked out the next morning, we headed to the airport having decided that driving to Liberia was out of the question due to distance and time constraints. While waiting on our delayed flight, I convinced the group to create a "to do" list by categories. Both the housing and industry projects would require experienced project managers. For good measure, one local manager and one African American manager. Fatou volunteered to research salary expectations in West Africa. Obviously, Natu would serve as the local manager. We also decided that the homes would be sold, not rented, to the residents to ensure stability and the benefits of "pride of ownership." I expressed that most of those relocating would probably be first time homeowners. After I said that, each of us got caught up with emotion understanding that our efforts would actually make dreams come true. A few tears dropped from my eyes knowing what it would mean to the people relocating to own their own new, modern homes. Always the pragmatic, Fatou said, "The market value of the homes will increase over time resulting in equity since they won't have mortgages because the housing costs are borne by the sponsors." Fatou told the group, "Discrimination against blacks trying to buy homes and obtain mortgages was legal during the decades of the residential building boom of the 1930's through 1970's in America resulting in generational wealth for whites and a pattern of renting and housing insecurity for blacks. Hopefully, our program starts a trend across Africa that results in generational wealth and stability for both Africans and re-locating African Americans." We all nodded in agreement, simultaneously fighting feelings of anger and hope at the same time.

As we waited, Kofi told us about a lecture he attended which condemned the tendencies of older adults to ignore the needs of future generations as if the world would end with them. Whether by abusing the earth, ignoring climate change or chronic budget deficits, the lecturer said that we have collectively failed to consider the needs of future generations. Kofi hoped out loud that our program would catch on and provide a template for all African nations since the future of our children requires us to create industry, jobs and mass home construction.

Natu listened and agreed with much of what he heard, but he didn't think we fully understood the mindset of some Africans. He said, "I don't mean to be negative, but it may not be as easy as you think to persuade our leaders to adopt your plans and ways of doing things. For one thing, too many of our people are comfortable with the few having nearly all the wealth and the masses having nothing. Some of us will kill thousands in order to stay in power and control wealth. Some of us leave "office" and take the coffers of the treasury with us leaving the nation bankrupt and in desperate condition. So, overcoming that mindset will not be easy and you have to be aware that everyone will not understand or like what you are trying to do." Somewhat deflated, we collectively sighed.

To show Natu that we understood, I said, "I hear you brother. I thought about all of that to be honest with you. I think the best course of action will be to establish programs only in regions where we are welcome and where there is no resistance whatsoever. That is our best chance for success." The others nodded in agreement. I noticed that Natu held his gaze on me with interest. Unable to look away, I returned the stare until I became self-conscious. I wondered to myself if he was interested in me? I could not deny that I found him very attractive. First

Darius, now crushing on Natu, I spilled out a laugh as I called myself a 'thirsty huzzie' in my head. Thankfully, the others didn't seem to notice.

Once we reached Monrovia, we checked into a multi-level hotel called "Hotel Africa." The hotel pool was in the shape of the continent of Africa with a bar with stools in the shallow water! The group decided to have a free rest of the day and agreed to meet in the morning before the Noon meeting with community leaders. Jet setters Kofi and Fatou had plans to visit with local friends. I was invited but decided to get some rest and stay on hotel grounds. Soon after getting my room key, I put on my swimsuit, fascinated by the pool with a bar inside, and headed outdoors.

To my surprise, Natu was sitting at the bar in the pool enjoying a cocktail. Shyly, I approached Natu and said, "Is this seat taken?" Natu smiled brightly and said "No." He told me that he had hoped I would come down after I got settled in. He took my hand and helped me into the pool and sparks of electricity rumbled between us at the touching and I felt we both knew it. Since he had been to Liberia several times, Natu told me about the best restaurants, landmarks and beaches. I asked him if he had a family in a sly attempt to find out if he was attached. Natu smiled knowingly and explained that, since last year, he had been separated from his wife of thirty years. Disappointed to learn he was married, I prepared myself for his story. Inwardly, I admitted to myself that I had become quite attracted to Natu, God help me. Tall, dark and handsome with chiseled, masculine features, he was easy on the eyes and was also intelligent and sincere. I should have known someone would be able to claim him.

Natu spoke and pulled me out of my momentary self-pity saying, "She told me that she filed for divorce in Dakar, but I have not seen the papers. She is from a wealthy local family and was no longer satisfied with our lifestyle since I refused to live off her family." A bit relieved, I said, "Do you have any children?" He told me about his son and daughter, both adults. In kind, I told him about Hassan and his family. Now his turn to grill me, he said, "I hope you don't mind me asking, but are you married or involved with someone?" I held up my left hand without a ring on it and said, "Does that answer your question?" "Not really," he said with a smile in his eyes, "since you don't have to be married to be involved with someone." I chuckled at that and said, "No, I am not involved with anyone," but I was too embarrassed to tell him how long it had been since I had been. After that, we talked about our lives attempting to convey to each other who we were. After a couple of hours, I told Natu I was going to go to my room and rest a while before dinner. Natu asked me if we could eat together that evening and I agreed to do so giving him a big, sincere smile.

In my room, I fell prostrate on my bed, giddy with excitement. A gorgeous, kind man was interested in me and I liked him back. Was he the presence I felt that night on the balcony at Victoria's? I made a pact with myself though to avoid getting involved with him, emotionally or physically, until he was divorced. Men have played that, "I'm separated" game for years at the expense of vulnerable women. I wasn't about to become a statistic, especially not now when I was about to embark on what I realized was my lifelong God given mission. Regardless, I *did* have to eat. I looked in the mirror and thought I had done very well with my "come back" plan. I slipped into a little, black dress without my girdle and without a wig. My "crowning glory" was full and beautiful in its natural grandeur. I looked in the mirror again and said, "You go!"

Natu drove us to a stand-alone restaurant in the middle of town. The ambiance was formal and romantic decorated in different shades of purple all over the room. When I stepped out of the car, Natu inhaled and looked at me with an expression of deep longing. I nearly forgot to breathe the look was so potent. Once again, we held glances and seemed unable to break away. We both knew something was happening between us. Unbeknownst to me, Natu had decided not to make any moves until he was officially divorced nor before we really got to know each other.

We were both a little nervous probably trying to avoid saying something stupid, so we quietly enjoyed our dinner of grilled chicken and potatoes. Natu said, "Karima, I am really impressed that this great idea came to you and that you actually had the courage to pursue it." Seeing that he had recognized a pivotal dilemma from early in the process, I was happy to explain. I responded, "To tell you the truth, I am too. I really took my time in deciding whether to pursue it since I had other business concepts I was also considering. This idea, however, just would not die no matter what else I thought about. Once I shared it with Fatou, it just started to come together so naturally. I have noticed for years that when something is consistent with God's plan, everything falls into place and basically, that's what is happening." "You are so right about that," Natu declared. After that, we fell into an easy conversation about our lives each telling the other the short versions of our journeys. Natu, emboldened by the natural vibe between the two of us said, "Karima, you are lovely in every way and I would really love to get to know you better." Believing that I needed to set some standards, I responded, "I would love that as well, but I have to admit that I would feel a lot more enthusiastic about it once your divorce goes through." "I completely understand," he said attentively. Having expressed our mutual interest, we slow danced to three songs and enjoyed the ambiance of the romantic setting until we left to return to the hotel, to separate rooms. I was glad to get back to the safety of my room because that slow dancing with Natu nearly killed me it was so powerfully intimate and provocative. The man is a threat to my rational thinking I realized.

The meeting the next day resulted in an agreement, subject to funding, to sell one thousand acres of government owned, forestland to the program for industry and housing. The land was located about one hundred miles north of Monrovia, the capital city of Liberia. Replete with uncut lumber despite that many of the trees had been sapped for rubber, there would be enough timber to supply both the mills and for residential housing. Housing construction would not commence in rural Liberia until after the mill was functional.

During the meeting with the Liberian leaders, Kofi received a call that required his early return to the States. Fatou and I decided not to go ahead to Ghana without him. Tickets were purchased at a local travel agency for flights from Monrovia to London to JFK, then to our respective final destinations of Phoenix and Atlanta. On the curbside at the airport, Natu held me as long as he could without calling attention to us. He told me how much he had enjoyed my company and that he would anxiously await my return. To set a stake in the future, he added, "I don't know where this will lead, but I want you to know that you have become special to me in the short time I've known you. I would like to be able to call you while you are away." "I would absolutely love to stay in touch with you because I feel a connection to you as well, I responded." We hugged again and I turned and walked into the terminal with cloudy eyes after giving him my numbers. Fatou and Kofi sensed that something was going on, but they didn't pry. Natu entered the terminal and looked at me until he couldn't see me anymore. At one point before that happened, I looked back and the connection of our hearts was sealed.

CHAPTER 17

Spirit

"This is what the Lord Almighty, the God of Israel, says to all those I carried into exile from Jerusalem to Babylon. Build houses and settle down. Plant gardens and eat what they produce. Marry and have sons and daughters; find wives for your sons and give your daughters in marriage so that they too may have sons and daughters. Increase in numbers there; do not decrease. Also seek the peace and prosperity of the city to which I have carried you into exile. Pray to the Lord for it, because if it prospers, you too will prosper. Do not let the prophets and diviners among you deceive you. Do not listen to the dreams you encourage them to have. They are prophesying lies to you in my name. I have not sent them," declares the Lord. **Jeremiah 29: 5-9.**

I could not have imagined that my beloved Karima would act out my dreams for our people. All this time, I have been able to stay of good cheer no matter the degree of calamity because I trusted in the sovereign power of God and in the safety of his control. Through his divine plan, my descendants are finding their way back home. We have suffered immeasurably as a people, but despite the denial and near erasure of our history, it is known that we had our day. "Our day" lasted thousands of years and we developed the world's earliest and most advanced civilization of that time. No amount of theft, nose chipping or misappropriation could deny it as the evidence of the same is still with us today.

Yet, we are not unscathed by our past, but we can take solace in the relentless efforts of our ancestors to fight for their land over and over again. We can also be assured by the fact that we survived, because a weaker group would not have. Despite what we have been told about ourselves as Africans, and just like the scattered Africans of the Americas, our people did not just lay down and take it, they fought back, a fact conveniently left out of history which prefers to paint us as docile, ignorant and compliant, basically content with our unfathomable predicament.

During Karima's time, European museums and archaeologists began to admit that Africans engineered the novel scientific, engineering, mathematical, architectural and medical developments during the first dynasties and beyond of Ancient Egypt. That the previous historical and published accounts of Egyptian and Nubian empires were bent towards a Eurocentric viewpoint which denied the truth of our true role as the creators of Ancient Egypt, one of the greatest and most powerful civilizations in the history of the world that lasted for over 3000 years, is of no surprise. Why would European colonialists, who needed to portray and treat African people as ignorant, illiterate, and lost savages solely to justify their rape and pillage of Africa's rich resources, ever want to give credit to Black people as being the first architects of high civilization? Ironically, the Greek and Roman historians and anthropologists of *ancient* times, the ones who actually came in contact and interacted with Ancient Egypt, told the truth about African and Ethiopian roles in Egypt and other African kingdoms from the start, but their findings were later intentionally misinterpreted, disregarded and discredited in favor of purposeful eradication of the truth.

Not even the diabolical, evil spirited objective to rewrite history however could destroy us and break our spirits since, no matter where the ships scattered abducted Africans, we managed to not only survive, but also found a way to dominate culturally and still contribute meaningfully to society wherever we were planted. Despite every effort to stunt our growth, we created novel art forms such as jazz and rock and roll and were inventors, originators and innovators. Even our slang and street style are of such high quality that they are copied and exploited regularly, turning up in commercials in warp speed. I don't mention rap since Africans have done that for centuries. After our people were taken off the continent and brought to the Americas, we entertained, invented and triumphed in every imaginable arena with the least amount of support and resources. When we learn to value black unity, which other cultures practice unapologetically, and develop a higher regard for the greater good, rejecting the "getting mine" mentality, we as a people will be able to recapture some of our past glory.

I follow Karima's story from afar because her audacious courage to follow her dream will change the course of the lives of generations of Africans. I pray the good Lord allows me to witness the ultimate reconciliation, the promise of Karima's program.

PART THREE

Not Unscathed

CHAPTER 18

Patrice

I looked around the dark, dank room and wondered where I was, but this was not the first time I had woken up in an unfamiliar place, disheveled and in a hazy state of mind. There was no point in theatrics or playing the victim. I knew why I was there, wherever it was. Drugs. I just could not beat my habit. I couldn't believe that I allowed drugs to cause my mother to take my child from me. After that, my urges became even worse. I take everything and anything to numb my mind, but still cannot forget the face of my baby girl the last time I saw her. Aliyah is three years old now, and my mother still will not allow me to see the baby.

Looking around again, I saw a dark figure coming in my direction and the Holy Spirit told me, "Leave now!" I quickly grabbed my backpack and ran as fast as I could, my track and field background kicking in clutch. Once I got out onto the streets, the events of the past twenty hours began to reveal themselves to me. The pattern was not new. I had "bartered" my body, every orifice, for drugs. When it was done, I felt like less than trash. Sometimes, they didn't even give me the drugs after I "performed", but what was I going to do, call the police? I walked out onto the Baltimore streets and was nearly blinded by the sunlight. Accustomed to people avoiding eye contact with me, I saw a woman looking at me with concern. I kept it moving not in the mood for a do-gooder or an undercover cop. The woman, a middle-aged black woman, crossed the street and walked towards me. When she reached me, she said, "Good morning Sister, I'm Sister Daly from Christ the Servant Church. I want you to know that you are a princess and the daughter of the Most High God and you deserve more from life than what you are getting." I just looked at her with a blank, deadpan stare. I turned around and started walking in the other direction. Sister Daly followed me and said, "Young Sister, let me help you with a hot meal, a bed, a program and any other need you may have." I kept walking, but there was something about Sister Daly that felt sincere to me, not just the rehearsed jargon of a holy roller. I slowed down unconsciously and when Sister Daly caught up with me she said, "Let's just go and eat together, OK?" I surprised myself when I nodded affirmatively.

We walked together to the diner on the corner. Sister Daly told me that she was a part of a street missionary program at her church that looks for people who are open to doing better. They help the people get to the root cause of their challenges and work with them to overcome their demons. She said, "When I saw you this morning, I saw such pain in your face and I wanted to see if I could help in some way." I spoke for the first time saying, "I want to see my baby," and then I let a dam of tears flow. Sister Daly moved to the seat next to me and held me even though I didn't look or smell very good. After that, we ate together in silence, but the atmosphere had changed from strain and unfamiliarity to co-existence and tolerance. I scarfed the food down, but Sister Daly said she could tell I had some home training by the way I consumed the food. Sister Daly asked me what the barriers were preventing me from seeing my daughter. I told her, "My daughter lives with my mother, but I am not allowed to see her until I am drug free. To get my child back, I would have to have a suitable home, finances enough to take care of a child, plus sobriety." Sister Daly told me about a Christian program where I could get not only supportive drug rehabilitation, but other resources as well to help get me on my feet. I was ready to say thanks for the meal and walk out, but something told me to hold still. Having been brought up in the church, I knew a phony from a person with God in them. In a hushed, pleading tone, I heard myself say, "Please help me Sister Daly. I'm ready."

Four months later, I walked out of my mother's home with Aliyah. I had graduated from the program clean and of sound mind. God had been restored as the head of my life and the Blood of Jesus ensured forgiveness of my sins. While in the program, I had learned that my mother's diabetes and high blood pressure had morphed into heart disease that was uncontrolled. My mother, Clara Simmons, was having a very hard time taking care of Aliyah. My mother had never taken the matter to court, so she never got any assistance for raising Aliyah and there was no court order standing between me and my mother.

When I first re-appeared on my mother's doorstep two weeks ago, my mother was shocked, but there was no doubt in her mind that I was clean and sober. Aliyah stood right behind Mom, holding her leg looking happy and healthy. She had no idea who I was since she had not seen me since she was a baby. By the time that first visit was over, Aliyah was calling me, "Mommy." I just thanked the Lord for answering my prayer and for his goodness.

Aliyah was the spitting image of me with caramel colored skin, bright, expressive eyes and a beautiful, wide smile. She is talkative and inquisitive. Everyday since that first day, I regularly came by to visit or take Aliyah out and our bond grew stronger. One day, Mom told me that I could take Aliyah once I was able to because she was feeling less and less well. She added that she needed to sell her house and move to senior housing soon because the house was too big for her to manage. Although overjoyed about taking Aliyah, I was equally concerned about my mother's health. Mom was only sixty-two years old, much too young to be sick from preventable diseases.

I told Mom that Aliyah could stay with me at the women's program while I waited to come up on the waitlist for independent housing. I continued, "Mom, I am going to tell you about something that will sound crazy at first, but maybe we need to think about it." Mom said, "Speak my child." I went on, "It's a modern day Back-to-Africa program where you are guaranteed a small house and a job. I heard about it at church and I know a few people who plan to sign up. You don't lose your American citizenship if you don't like it and don't want to stay. Since Dad passed, it's just you, Aliyah and me. I am an only child; you are an only child and Aliyah is an only child. We have no one but us and we are just surviving here, nothing more. Over there, we would not be minorities. They make sure you have a job and give you a house free of charge because it's part of your program fees which are paid for by donors. I feel like you could get your health back under less stress and Aliyah could grow up in a place where she is not constantly told, in one way or the other, that she is less than. What do we have to lose?" Mom was silent, but still listening. For the next few days, we continued to discuss and marinate on the idea. Mom was a bit hesitant based upon all the diseases and starvation she'd heard about in Africa.

Patrice didn't know that, on her own, Clara was thinking about it and decided not to share with Patrice that she was researching West Africa for her own peace of mind. Clara did everything from reading, to Internet searches, to "YouTube" videos and was positively impacted by what she learned. West Africa was mostly stable and she could now see them settling there. Clara eventually told Patrice about the things she learned and they decided to relocate through the "Motherland Bound" program. Clara also asked Patrice to move back in.

Once I was settled back in my mother's home, we worked together to settle local affairs and started packing, determined to take items we wouldn't expect to find in West Africa. Mom decided not to sell her house so that she would have some rental income and just in case we came back to the States. That morning, Mom prepared a classic, southern breakfast for us including grits, biscuits, sausage, scrambled eggs, coffee and juice for baby. We enjoyed the meal immensely and were all keenly aware of the new positive atmosphere in the house. I prayed silently and then said, "We have a lot to be thankful for Mom. For one, I never thought I would see this day, but the Lord was on my side. The morning I walked out of that "den," not wanting to be too graphic in front of the child, a big, unfamiliar figure was fastly approaching me, but I was too quick for him and got out to the streets. Deep in my soul, I knew he would have ......" Then, I fell silent. "Our prayers for you were not in vain," Clara said. "Let's get this cleared up so we can keep working on our plans," I said, wanting to change the subject. Moments later, I grabbed my mother's hand saying, "Mom, I don't know if you noticed, but I didn't eat the sausage or the eggs." Mom nodded affirmatively. "Please don't take this the wrong way," I pleaded, "but I learned the health benefits of a plant based diet in the program. Turns out the protein we get from animals is secondary protein because they get it from the plants they eat. That means we don't need to eat meat to get proteins, we can get them directly from plants. I won't bother you with it now, but it may be the answer to eliminate most of your health conditions." "I have heard something about that you know, but with you "being away," I couldn't add any more challenges to my plate, but maybe now I can try to work up to it," Mom said. "I'm only sixty two years old and I plan to make the best of this whole opportunity we are embarking on. I know they have open produce markets over there, so we should be able to sustain it," she added. Incredibly excited by that point, I replied, "We could also plant our own garden or sponsor a community garden." With renewed enthusiasm for our collective futures, we continued packing earnestly, like we had some place to go.

CHAPTER 19

Anthony

I took a drag of my blunt as I sat on top of a picnic table by myself at the Toro Park in Decatur, Georgia. I don't smoke weed regularly, but I needed something to calm my nerves. I wondered to myself how my life could have turned out this way. Although only 26 years old, as I sat on that park table, I looked back to my high school days when I was a popular, NBA bound, college athlete. Back then, I felt like I had the world at my feet. Girls on demand, dudes wanting to be my boy, heck, even the teachers favored me and made life easy for me, I recalled. At six feet, seven inches, I always stand out in the crowd, unless I'm in the gym. When I was recruited to a big ten university, I believed the NBA was within my reach. It was not to be though because of a meniscus tear in my second year of college. Even so, after sitting out a year for rehabilitation, I accepted an offer to play in Eastern Europe. It wasn't the NBA, but the pay was good and all the travel and perks made me feel like I was a success. Although I never got the "G" League call I had hoped for while in Serbia, I was content with the life I was living between Europe and the States. I became a man during those years and had grown sophisticated in my tastes and had expectations for my life.

Fate intervened once again by way of a second meniscus tear and I reluctantly returned to Atlanta. With no real job skills besides playing or coaching, I wondered if I could get a good job to pay my share of the bills at Mom's house once my savings were gone. Since I've been back, I avoid contact with high school and neighborhood friends because I feel like a loser not having met their expectations for my life. I didn't want to have to explain why I didn't go "pro" or have some other role in the league. They wouldn't get that, in Europe, I had played professionally. I've been back in the States a month already and haven't even told my father that I am back out of shame. Things went from bad to worse when my girlfriend, Monica, told me that she intentionally miscarried our baby by taking a pill because, to her, neither of us had the resources to raise a child. Soon after that, I lost her too because I would never forgive her for being so shallow and for what she did to our unborn child. The way I'm feeling right now has a lot to do with that. That was my baby, my child that I would never know because she made a decision for the both of us. I'm no psychiatrist, but I believe I am still mourning the death of my child on top of everything else.

All by myself at the park, I just shook my head in disbelief of it all. I thought to myself, this reefer must be spiked because I'm starting to think about that Back-to-Africa program Coach Anderson told me about. Coach also told me that he heard the NBA was starting a league in Africa. Moving to Africa would be an extreme thing to do, but I just want to get away. A week ago, I was stopped by the police for a tail light issue that ended with me being face down on the sidewalk and searched. My friends have been through worse. Staying in America was starting to feel dangerous. At least in West Africa, you wouldn't have to fear racial discrimination.

As the days passed, even though I felt like I was tripping. I kept thinking about Africa. I was not one of those Blacks who saw Africa as a wasteland or something to be ashamed of; people always seem to be confused as to who should be ashamed. I'm already accustomed to international travel and living abroad. I'm a citizen of the world and Africa is the homeland of my people. I would love to live there, for a while at least. I decided to go and talk to my mother, "Mrs. Alice Wright" as her friends called her, about it and she saw nothing but potential and opportunity for me. "How many former professional basketball players would there be in Africa that the NBA could call upon?" she asked. She suggested I speak to my father, "Mr. Jack Wright, about it as well.

I hadn't even let my father know about the second injury, let alone that I was back. I just could not face the anticipated disappointment in his eyes. I called him anyway like Mother suggested and we agreed to meet for breakfast. My mother allegedly forgot to tell me that she told him I was back. My dad and I are close, but we argued the last time we spoke about my lack of pursuit of G league opportunities. Like a lot of young brothers, my father had taught me everything I knew and my Dad was emotionally invested in my success, a little too much. He wanted his son in THE league, period, and felt that I had been in Europe long enough.

We met outside a local restaurant and hugged a long time before we went in. I told Dad everything. He finally spoke saying, "I felt like something was wrong when I didn't hear from you. I know we argued the last time we spoke, but you still should have called me when you got back." I nodded in agreement allowing my father to continue speaking. "That's all in the past now Son and it seems you have stumbled upon another blessing. I think you should go, but the league opportunity may not present itself for a while," Dad concluded. I cheered up and thanked him for his support. Jack added, "Remember this too Son, if your residency is over there, you might even be able to play in that league once that knee heals for good." Overjoyed, I thought that absolutely nothing better had ever been said to me in my whole life.

Later that evening, I was looking at a game and a commercial came on announcing the start of an NBA program in Africa. I shot up from the couch and said, this is it! A sign from God. I decided to get in touch with the Coach to get more info on the Back-to-Africa program. If he could get me into the Motherland Bound program and I relocate, maybe, just maybe, I could get involved with the NBA over there.

CHAPTER 20

King and Queen

Charles King was in deep thought. He had to find something for himself and Bridgette to eat. Going through this is getting harder and harder he thought. "Bridgette, come over for a second," he yelled. Bridgette Clark, Charles' lady, came near him and smiled. Bridgette thought, I can never get enough of looking at this handsome, strong man. He was about six feet tall with wavy black hair, mocha colored skin and bedroom eyes. Even though we were homeless and living on the streets, we were committed to each other. Charles broke into my trance saying, "Do you want to get a burger or put a salad or something together from the dollar store?" Placing my index finger on my chin, I jokingly said, "Why I prefer sirloin from Andre's and a baked potato with the works." Charles sighed and said, "One day, baby, one day." After that, we walked over to the dollar store spending about ten dollars on our food stamps card and went back to our tent.

About two months ago, a program purchased a lot from the City and set up an encampment for the homeless population. Charles and I were approved to pitch a tent and live here and we are able to sleep at night without fear, finally. It was a great improvement from our previous "lifestyle," I recalled. Here, there is a security guard at night watching the tents and there are common areas with toilets and showers. Still, I thought to myself, how low do you have to be to think that living in a tent is a good thing?

After they settled in for the evening, Charles said, "Bridgette, honey, I am so sorry for all of this. You are a classy, good woman and I can't even afford to make sure you have clean clothes to wear. You're forty-five years old and I'm fifty-one. Our health isn't that bad. Maybe we should try and work again and get a place?" Charles believed that his more positive thinking was a result of getting sleep at night since they had moved into the encampment. Bridgette sighed and looked at Charles saying, "You may be right Charles, but I don't blame you for any of this. We met on the streets, so I was down on my luck too when I met you. I, and a lot of other people went from home ownership, to divorce, to an apartment, to weekly rentals, to renting a room, to couch surfing, to self-medication and landing on the streets. I must say, I'm also sick of this kind of life, but at least I finally got into a healthy relationship," and she laughed robustly. Joining her in laughter, Charles admired Bridgette's short, wavy hairstyle and her youthful, brown, pretty face. She was always in a good mood and smelled good no matter what, he thought.

He recalled meeting her in a line for homeless services. Back then, it was all fairly new to him. He recounted his story to Bridgette again saying, "My son's mother, Shay, put me out for quitting another job. I had just paid our rent and had no savings. My family lives in New York, but even if I had gone back, there was no one to stay with. My first night without a roof over my head, I stayed in my car, but my height pretty much ruled out trying that for a second night. I just walked around the downtown area and eventually found places to sleep, if you call waking up every twenty minutes sleep. I didn't have a way to pay my phone bill or to feed myself, so I sold my car. After that, I stayed in weekly hotels for about a month, then I ran out of money again. Getting another job seemed impossible since I couldn't even shower or brush my teeth consistently. I went to that homeless services event looking for any kind of help I could get. Didn't get much from them, but I found my Queen." "And

I, my King", Bridgette responded. They talked about their lives more and then fell asleep.

The following Monday, they both went to a job and resource fair targeted to their "demographic." Dressed in good quality thrift store finds that were straight out of the cleaners, they almost looked out of place in that kind of setting. After about six robo-interviews each, they saw a table from a local church. Looking at each other like, "It's time," they walked over together and talked with the representative. Noticing pamphlets about Africa, Charles picked one up and put it in his pocket.

When they got back to the tent, they settled down on the reinforced foam mattress bolstered by layers of blankets and talked about the day, surmising they would at least get a few second interviews. After two weeks passed with no calls at all, they resigned themselves to more pain and suffering. They both felt so defeated that they pondered buying wine. Both had past drinking problems, so they resisted despite their strong feelings of despair and loss of hope. Later that evening, Charles said, "You know that pamphlet I got from the church people that day?" Bridgette nodded. "Would you believe it was about a Back-to-Africa program," he said incredulously. Bridgette said, "Nah, you joshing me!" He said, "No, I'm not. On top of that, it says everybody gets a job and a house when they get there and they can keep their American citizenship through dual citizenship rights." They looked at each other, shook their heads and laughed as if to say it was crazy thinking.

The next morning, Bridgette looked at Charles and said, "Baby, maybe we should look into it." Knowing what she was talking about, he said, "I dreamed we were there last night. Let's go ahead and look into it." After breakfast of bananas and granola, they decided to visit the Motherland Bound local office. Taking rail transit downtown, they were there by ten. After meeting the staff person named Lola Waite, they asked all of their questions and got all the information they needed. Charles proudly told the lady about his job history in sales and about Bridgette's history in retail. Lola assured them they had transferable skills that would be marketable. Bridgette asked what they had to pay if they wanted to be a part of it. Lola responded, "You pay nothing. All of the costs are paid by grants for those relocating. The first group leaves in March. First come, first serve as long as you are of African American heritage." Charles asked to confer with Bridgette privately and Lola left the room to give them privacy. "What do we have to lose?" he asked. "As long as we can leave if we don't like it, I'm okay. But what about your son?," Bridgette asked. "If I can turn my life around, he will be the better off for it and we can come back here when we please," he said. "Let's do it then," said Bridgette, and they became relocators numbers 49 and 50. With just one month before March 15th, they left to get vital records for expedited passports.

That night, they completed a "things to do" list together. Bridgette didn't have any close family except for her mother who was not speaking to her at the time. Bridgette decided to call her anyway. Her mother was shocked by the news but didn't object only saying, "Anything is better than what you're doing right now." She also requested that Bridgette make sure to come and see her before she left and insisted Bridgette give her an address when they landed and settled in.

Charles just texted his family and friends not fully disclosing the long-term nature of his plans. He did, however, go to see his son, Jr., and told him he would be gone for a while, but would be back. His son cried and it tore Charles apart at the thought of missing his son's childhood. Remembering to stay strong, he reminded his son that he would be back in the summer to see him and Little Man cheered up. Charles left his son that day determined to redeem himself. He never told anyone, not even Bridgette, that he lost his last job for stealing. It was just too embarrassing to admit and proved to be a barrier to future employment. He had to re-build his name and his character and would be doing it in the "cradle of civilization," a good omen to say the least.

A week before they left, Bridgette showed Charles that she had $2,500.00 her mother had given her. They agreed to keep it close to the vest in case they needed it for any reason. Charles also told Bridgette that his brother was going to send him something as well before they left. They toasted their adventure with sparkling cider to avoid relapsing at a bad time. "My Queen, I will do everything in my power to protect you and to deserve you," Charles promised. "My King, I trust you with my life. Let's go and become who God intended us to be," Bridgette pledged.

CHAPTER 21

Simone

"I need to do something to get my mind off Darius Jones," Simone thought, as she browsed at a local boutique. We met for dinner last night at a popular seafood restaurant at his request. He had called me about a week ago while the other board members were in Africa. He said he wanted to get to know me and talk about the project. Not thinking twice about it, I agreed to meet him Saturday afternoon.

Thinking back on it, I wish I had declined because the meeting was a little uncomfortable. The restaurant itself was modern and airy and had a great reputation. We sat down and conversed easily at first. He seemed forthright and enthusiastic about Karima's program. Then, he said he wasn't so sure about the overall business concept. He asked me, "Do you condone discrimination?" "Of course not," I replied." Anticipating my response, he casually said, "That's what I feel like we're doing by not giving everyone the chance to go." To my surprise, I heard myself say, "I can see what you mean."

After that, we talked about our families and I told him that my sons are both attending Xavier University in New Orleans. "We're very proud of them," I added. Darius frowned slightly and said, "I didn't realize you were married." "Why not," I responded. "I just assumed you were not since most black women are heads of households," he said smugly. "Well, I happen to know hundreds of nuclear black families from my work in the schools," I responded, slightly offended. After that, Darius just glared at me with a question in his eyes, but didn't say anything. For good measure, I flashed my pear shaped diamond ring in his face and we both laughed, but I wondered in my head how he had missed it.

Nothing really went wrong at the meeting *per se*. I just felt funny possibly getting into a situation where I'm not in agreement with Karima who brought me onto the board. During our meal, Darius and I did get to know each other better, which is a good thing. He spoke lovingly of his wife and his daughter and added that he "would hate to feel anyone discriminated against them because of their skin color." Returning to the discussion of the program, I said, "Darius, it's not discrimination in this kind of situation. Your family can move wherever they wish to at any time, but this program is to address a profound historical event and to perhaps change the ending." "Simone," he responded, "Our troubled history is all the more reason this program should be the last one to reject people." I was starting to wonder if he had a point.

CHAPTER 22

Darius

"Gotcha," Darius uttered when he got into his Mercedes G Wagon after having dinner with Simone. "Two members likely voting my way and one to go!" I had thought I might have to romance Simone to get her vote until she said she was married. I chuckled to myself and thought, "She ain't fine enough for me to be fighting over." Nonetheless, I felt like Simone could see the error in judgment on the part of the founders. I didn't ask her to vote with me, but the groundwork was laid and I have the feeling I can count on her support at the next meeting.

Once Kofi, Karima and Fatou return, I plan to call an emergency meeting to have them address my "legal concerns." Doing my homework while they're abroad, I met with my attorney friend from college, Keith Harris, for a consultation. Keith told me, "The group can proceed with a special interest program although it cannot be supported by certain federal funds or federal benefits." I knew I had struck out on that point since "rainmaker" Kofi would seek private donations. All was not lost though because Keith was going to research a narrow legal issue for me that might throw a wrench in their plans if I don't get the majority vote I need at the next meeting.

In the meantime though, I decided to continue to canvass Karima and Simone to get a majority vote regarding inclusiveness. If I can't, it will pave the way for them to proceed as they envisioned. "I'm not going to allow that to happen though, no matter what," I decided. "If it does, I'll find a way to make them all pay for trying to elevate people whose lifestyles are synonymous with crime and strip club morality."

Kofi, nor anybody else in my life knew that I had been raised from fourteen years old in foster care. It is a closely guarded secret that I am incredibly ashamed of. I allowed myself to remember. For years, I told people my parents died in a car accident when I was young and that my grandparents raised me after that. Of course, to keep my story straight, I had to kill off both my parents and grandparents so as not to have to explain their absence in my life now. The truth is, my father abandoned us early in childhood and my mother got strung out on drugs and was prostituting herself for drugs. The state stepped in and removed us from her home when I was fourteen, that part was true. I was placed in the home of Ed and Diane Smith. My sister, Marilyn, was also removed from the home, but we were separated and I have not seen her since that day. The Smiths were a church going, stable couple who did not want children of their own, but fostered abused and neglected children out of a sense of duty. I was very grateful to have good food, a clean bedroom and basic stability after being placed with the Smiths. Even so, I still worried about Marilyn and my mother from time to time.

Mr. Smith was a son's dream, I recalled fondly. He taught me to love sports, to speak well and to love country. I didn't take to Mrs. Smith as much and it wasn't her fault. She just reminded me of what mothers were capable of. My mother had been the love of my life before she started using drugs. I just cannot forgive her for destroying our lives, so I had ill feelings towards her and anyone who looked like her. I pretended to adore Mrs. Smith though because I didn't want to lose points with Mr. Smith.

Despite finding stability for myself, I missed my sister and still wonder to this day what became of her. I entertained looking for her at one time, but I'm still not ready to face my past. How would I tell my wife and child about her when I never told them I had a sister? I came back to my right mind. I've put too much distance between my beginnings and my life now. I cannot risk it by digging them up.

CHAPTER 23

Karima

A lot had happened in the five months since our return from West Africa. To my delight, I spoke to Natu regularly and we are getting to know each other very well. My next trip is scheduled for mid-March when I will travel to Senegal with the first group of relocators. Soon after our return from Africa five months ago, Kofi raised over six hundred thousand dollars thereby exceeding the five hundred thousand matching grant requirement. The additional funds were pledged and paid for by doctors, actors, directors, sports figures, entrepreneurs and many allies who believe in the program. Kofi is continuing to build the coffers with a goal of twenty million dollars to assure the solvency and sustainability of our program.

Because Natu was in Senegal already, he was able to order and receive all the necessary lumber and building supplies in one month. His team had pre-fabricated wood and parts for the first fifty homes to comply with the deadline dictates of the matching grant. In fact, the homes would be ready for occupancy earlier than required. They were currently working on foundations for the first fifty houses which would be fully completed by February 28th.

A project manager from Baltimore, Bill Calloway, was hired and traveled to Senegal. He is currently working closely with Natu to get the industry projects off the ground as well. All payroll and administration are being originated in the States by direct deposit to Nafre's local bank. Too busy to become scared by the way God was allowing my dream to become reality, I stayed prayed up and focused. I had truly become a busy executive and had to schedule in family activity and "me time."

Soon after our return, I worked with Fatou to create a marketing and publicity campaign geared to find people wanting to relocate. We had long, self-searching conversations to come up with the right approach. Overall tone and optics were of utmost importance to avoid appearing condescending, angry, desperate or exploitive. We did all we could to convey the spirit of the effort, which was simply to offer an option to the children of the diaspora to return to the land of their forefathers and mothers.

We got it all done in a month, including the building of a website. Afterwards, slowly but surely, people started signing up. We plan to dispatch the first group of fifty on March fifteenth and the second group six months later. If more houses are needed after locals take their equal share, we will build more.

The only obstacle we'd had to deal with was Darius. I hadn't been in my home from the airport ten minutes upon my return from Africa when he called. He sounded winded and anxious and asked if I would meet him for dinner. Overwhelmed with jet lag and sleepiness, I told him, "Darius, let me call you tomorrow. I just walked in the door and I'm so tired I can't think." Sounding a little dejected, he said, "OK, talk to you then." My, how things change. I remembered the short lived attraction I had for Darius before I left, but it was quickly extinguished once I learned he was a married man. I wondered what he was up to calling me immediately upon my return.

Well, I found out the following week when I met him for dinner at a nearby Mexican restaurant. It was almost comical, I recalled. He was coming on like "Rico Suave" with the gushing compliments and flirtatious snarls. After a while, it started becoming annoying so I told him, "Look, Darius, I appreciate your compliments, but I am confused about your intentions because I know that you are married. Maybe it's me, but I need you to be clear about where you are coming from." Visibly taken aback, Darius tried to appear insulted and said, "I assure you I have no personal interest in you Karima. You asked me to be a part of this, I didn't seek you out. That's what's wrong with you sisters, always insulting a brother and thinking you're better than somebody. I give you a few compliments and you think I'm trying to get you in the bed." Righteously faux indignant, he added, "I happen to believe your mission is not legally sound and I wanted to confer with you personally, since it is your vision, in order to help you avoid problems, maybe even lawsuits."

It hit me like a ton of bricks, "This fool is crazy!" There was no mistaking that he was flirting aggressively, but it had nothing to do with romance. Having one of those powerful fan-blowing-you-backwards moments, I gathered myself. I said, "Darius, please don't insult my intelligence, we both know you were flirting and, secondly, our mission is entirely legal so I am not intimidated by your veiled threats. If your beliefs don't line up with our mission and our plans, feel free to resign immediately." He stood up and said, "Are you threatening me Karima, because if you are, you will regret it the rest of your life. I was trying to help your simple butt, but now I'll just take this in another direction. Please watch your messages for an emergency meeting of the Board," he said as he stormed out of the restaurant.

As soon as I got home, I called Fatou and Kofi and told them what happened. At that point, Kofi confessed that Darius had changed over the years and probably had not been a good choice for the board and the mission. He apologized for not speaking up when I mentioned him, but he said he never thought he was this far gone. Before, we hung up, we all got notice of Darius' request for an emergency meeting by email. Kofi, in turn, called the company attorney.

The meeting took place two days later at 1:00 p.m. in the Phoenix office. Fatou and Kofi, feeling it was important to appear in person, had landed that morning. All Board members arrived on time. The atmosphere was serious and somber, no joking or catching up with each other. I called the meeting to order as the Board Chairperson and Fatou took roll call. We wanted to do everything by the books in case homey tried to start something later. Then, I said, "Darius, you called this meeting, please state your business." He replied, "I move for a formal vote that any person, regardless of race, color or creed may apply to the program and be approved." I called for discussion. Since we all knew his angle, his motion was not a surprise. Kofi spoke up and reiterated that, "The entire purpose of the program is to address those who have been called, by Africans, 'the lost children', those taken off the continent as chattel for the sole purpose of slavery. The program is intended as a vehicle for those descendants of slaves to return to their ancestral home." Kofi's eloquent explanation almost moved us to tears. Even Darius seemed moved. Yet, he persisted replying, "Still, that does not give us the right to discriminate." No one else wanted to speak. I asked if anyone had comments for further discussion and, when no one responded, I called for the vote. "All in favor?" Darius said, "Aye." "All against?" Kofi, Fatou, myself and Simone raised our hands. I asked, "Any abstentions"? There being no one left to vote, there was no response to that question. "Alright then, the motion did not pass," I proclaimed.

Darius stood up and shook his head saying, "I can't believe you all could be so obtuse and narrow minded. Well, you may have won this vote, but you will not win the war. " I replied, "Darius, you may resign if you are so disgusted with the premise and purpose of this program." "Don't you dare think you will dismiss me like the fly Obama swatted the life out of. I will do everything in my power to right this ship. You will hear from me again. You clowns don't know who you're dealing with," he said as he walked out. We all exploded in laughter after he left. While his antics were very concerning, they were all so outrageous that it was very comical. Still in shock though, the rest of us left the office for the nearest watering hole to ponder our predicament. Without question, Darius Jones had become unhinged mentally somewhere along the way. Simone told the group about her dinner with him for the first time and no one was surprised by his attempts to manipulate her.

Fatou said, "We may need to get a background check on Mr. Jones in case he wants to play dirty. Apparently, he's spending a lot of time trying to change the entire basis on our program. Maybe there are things we don't know about him that may explain his determination to force his way." "You're right Fatou," said Kofi, "something does not add up. Even non-blacks would understand the premise even if they thought it was a bad idea to return to Africa. How can you discriminate against people who are already free to travel to Africa, live, buy property at whim?"

"I hate to say it, but a lot of blacks are just preoccupied with not ruffling feathers. They live in fear of offending other people who don't look like them, but have no problem offending other blacks. This has been happening for centuries. Darius strikes me as one of those people," I said, now totally understanding what Darius had been up to when we went out to dinner that time. Simone echoed my sentiment saying, "When I went out to dinner with him, he made a few comments that caught my attention. It was as if he had very low expectations for my life without even knowing me. I'm so glad I didn't get caught up with his agenda because I now see that he was trying to get me to vote his way." More relaxed after drinks, we decided as a group to proceed as planned without giving any energy to whatever he might be up to.

Thankfully, no one has heard from him since that Board meeting and that was almost five months ago. So much has happened since then, including securing funding and finding participants. I personally felt empowered and unafraid of Darius' threats because we'd met with our attorneys to ensure the legalities were air tight and compliant. We also knew that if he missed one more meeting we could vote him out, according to the by-laws, and that was the plan.

CHAPTER 24

Natu

Standing back, leaning on an upright shovel, Natu took a deep breath and took it all in not believing his fortune. Basking in the sunlight of the open fields and setting markers for foundations, he listened as the birds chirped and the insects buzzed. He wondered, how on earth do I deserve to take part in such a momentous project as to provide future homes for those on such a remarkable journey as the "children of the diaspora?" He never told Karima and the others how much in awe many Africans were of African Americans. There was a time when Africans, with their own struggles and challenges, felt hopeless and looked to Black Americans to redeem the race. We had seen the well-heeled, dignified American Blacks buying homes, going to church and sending their children to prestigious colleges and universities, many of them historically black institutions, in the 1960's and 1970's. Sadly though, our dreams to be redeemed by blacks in America died as we watched from afar the gains from the hard fought American civil rights period give way to broken families, rampant drug addiction and poverty in the 1980's. We also witnessed the formerly high ideals and standards of the group give way to what appeared to be a less civilized black culture where other things were valued and tolerated like over emphasis on material things, public denigration and rejection of black women and turning a blind eye to the struggles of the masses by "successful" blacks.

Many American Blacks, he also knew, didn't think much of Africans as a group either because they believe we sold them. Neither group really bothered to find out what really happened to us as a people which is sad, he thought. As a native son, Natu knew of the pain African's suffered fighting colonialism, disease, tribal conflict and too many languages. Merely trying to keep our land and sanity was a full time job, leaving little time to worry about the ones who were taken. In fact, most of the time, the ones taken away seemed a lot better off than us.

"Natu, what are the dimensions of the larger solar panels again," Bill Calloway asked him, breaking Natu away from his thoughts. "Sixty by sixty," he told him. The two men walked over to the hanger like structure where the solar panels were being assembled. They marveled at the productivity garnered from a team of ten men and themselves. Everything from ordering, to deliveries, to construction had gone without a hitch. In fact, the only problem they'd encountered, if you could call it that, were the inquiries from local residents wanting to occupy the homes themselves. Natu and Bill always referred them to the local "Motherland Bound" office where they could find out the requirements of the program and complete the application. Incredibly, it looked as if the supply and demand would be a close match, another miracle.

After work was done, Natu spent each evening the same way, thinking about Karima. He envisioned them walking together, laughing together and enjoying each other. He wanted to hold her tenderly and kiss her all over. Racier thoughts of them satisfying their carnal needs occurred more often than he cared to admit. He could not wait to tell her that he was legally divorced, but he would wait until he could tell her in person and show her the papers. He was literally relieved when Karima made it clear she would not become involved with him physically until his divorce was finalized. Usually, women let men have their way with them with few demands in return. It was almost boring. He had heard about the reputation of American women for being easy, but he was not able to confirm it by Karima. Like most men, he loved a challenge. It made him want to deserve her and to earn her love.

Both Natu and Bill each got permission to purchase one of the new homes since they too needed a home in the area. Each of them chose two bedrooms in case family traveled to Nafre to stay for a spell. Natu, however, was hoping for a permanent visitor, named Karima.

CHAPTER 25

Darius

After that emergency board meeting back in October, I really didn't know what to do. My attorney friend Keith came back with nothing I could use to dismantle the program. All this time, I've been racking my brain to come up with a plan to change the course of their mission. I considered everything from staging a media assault against them to expose the program on some bogus claim to using scare tactics against the other board members to run them off course. Finally, I realized an updated "divide and conquer" strategy was the way to go. I went to the "Motherland Bound" website and found out that a large group of fifty six people would fly out of JFK on a flight to Senegal on March fifteenth to settle the first fifty members of the program. Guess who's going to meet them there?

Since I'm a board member, they won't have any choice but to include me in their plans. I know for a fact that Africans don't trust American Blacks, so I will go straight to their African counterparts and "slip" them inside information on the exploitive intentions of the founders. I'll have the Africans thinking the Americans pulled a fast one on them designed to take their land because the Americans know there are minerals in the ground. By the time I finish with them, the Americans will be bounced out of Africa so fast they won't know what hit them.

Sometimes you have to fight fire with fire. They were able to head me off legally with their army of attorneys and advisers, but they will never anticipate my next move. Besides my foster parents and a few others through the years, I have never found people to be level headed or loyal. If my smear campaign doesn't work, I plan to have plenty of American dollars to buy allegiance to my agenda if need be. I will not have them think they ran me off like a two-dollar whore. My education, position and assets demonstrate my worth. How dare a bunch of bleeding hearts reject my advice, especially when I implored them to consider fair play and equality?

My wife has called me a sociopath for forcing my way after disagreements at home and at work. I feel like she's half joking, half on the level when she says that. As the man of the house, I am responsible for all of us, and therefore, I have the last word. I don't make all decisions though, because I'm a fair man. I let her dress our daughter and deal with the school. She cooks, shops and comes and goes as she pleases as long as I know where she is and what she is doing. She balked when I installed cameras inside the home accusing me of spying on her, but I was able to make her see it was just a security tool. When I review the daily tapes, I do sometimes feel a little voyeuristic watching her bathe and undress, but she doesn't know that I have seen her and the pool guy looking at each other. I don't know what she might do while I'm gone. Some of the cameras are well hidden and beyond any search she could employ if she got a mind to have them removed.

I don't consider my outside involvements adultery because, as a man, that is my right to do. I respect my wife, so I am very discreet and have not brought a problem into our home. I usually get what I want, from whom I want it, but as much as I would like to deny it, I still want Karima although she doesn't seem to be too interested in me. She is so innocent and beautiful. She has no idea what I can do for her. In Africa, there will be little security and police presence, I plan to make her mine and keep her for as long as possible. She will only be second to my wife.

CHAPTER 26

Elder Bunmi Whey

Hanging up the phone after a long conversation with Karima, I couldn't get the smile off my face. Every time we speak, I feel closer to Karima as a friend. As a member of the "Motherland Bound" advisory panel based in Senegal, I oversee operations for new residents, both Senegalese and African American, before and after they move into their homes. My responsibilities also include obtaining permits, arranging landscaping, choosing vendors for fixtures and appliances, purchasing standard furnishings and filling welcome baskets for each home. Preparing the baskets for each home with other villagers is pure joy. Of course, basics like toilet paper and towels are a given. The fun came from buying all the local supplies and treats such as custom doormats and home-made soaps. We also ordered a boatload of American staples such as pancake mix and spaghetti sauce. I assembled a team of twenty women to help me prepare each home to be move-in ready by March tenth, five days early.

Karima and Fatou wired all the funds to Nafre needed to prepare each home for occupancy. We have worked tirelessly to ensure the deadline of March fifteenth is met as promised. My twenty year old daughter, Kendall, turned out to have very good instincts when it came to interior design and proved instrumental to the project. She commissioned fabrics, rugs and wallpaper for the homes featuring traditional design, local designers, artists and artisans for the new homes.

Many of Nafre's young people are idle. Either they grow up and leave, go abroad for higher education and never return, or stay and lead a sedentary lifestyle since there are no jobs or ways to become productive. Although Karima's program is focused on American Blacks returning to the home of their forefathers, the program will be a blessing to our local community as well.

After I thought about it, I realized no new home had been built in Nafre since 1990 when Bola Cupps, a native son of Nafre, returned from Sierra Leone after a divorce. He built a small home from the ground up and still lives there. I have received twenty-two housing applications from local villagers. Most of them came from people between twenty-five and thirty six years of age. There are five hundred and two residents of Nafre and most of them live in family homes or buildings. The young people from those homes are anxious to strike out on their own. They will be able to also get jobs at the solar plant or the vineyards, which will last for years according to our projections. This rare opportunity means everything to the longevity of Nafre, which was destined to die out.

We had been asking the Lord for resources and help for our village and our people. Word traveled fast after those meetings with the Americans last fall. Although Africans can keep secrets, we didn't waste any time telling everybody what was going on. There was very little opposition from the villagers. The new jobs and housing easily sold the plan. We considered the program an answered prayer since we all needed something good to happen for us. Some older people did express fear of the new residents whose culture and habits would be different than ours. Bola reminded them that respect was due and told them that blacks in America drive popular culture all over the world with their talents and innovativeness, usually without the benefit of independent resources or support from lending institutions. Differences in social mores never bothered me because I knew their foundation was formed from our culture. For instance, both groups are relationship and family oriented. We all respect our Elders and honor no one above the true and living God. Surely, there will be differences and conflicts, but nothing the Elders could not work through. All of us will have mutual interest in the program not only working, but thriving.

Elder Tamu is working with a team of ten villagers on an orientation for the program. The Orientation will take place over one week with daily workshops covering everything from traditions, culture, expectations, government, food, entertainment, geography and home life. To ensure attendance, land titles will not be issued until the orientation is completed by the members. The Americans have been told about the mandatory orientation, so there will be no surprises. The classes will be taught in the same place we met with Karima, Kofi and Fatou back in the Fall.

Like I said, we can keep secrets when we want to and I have one. I am working with our premiere event planner, Fatima Chebo, to welcome the new residents home on a huge scale. We have invited nearby villagers from Senegal and Gambia to help us say, "Welcome Home!" We will have speakers, historians, food, music, traditional dancing, rappers, ribbons, balloons and every conceivable tool to make it the party of the century. After all, this may be the first official welcome event for the lost children to be held in modern times. We will use the Internet and other publicity tools to show the entire world that African descendants of the diaspora, members of the "lost tribe," have returned home, the ultimate reconciliation. We know that many descendants of Africans have returned on their own, but without recognition or anything close to the scale made possible by this program. Just thinking about it warms my soul. I ask the Lord every day to make the celebration the success I know it can be.

CHAPTER 27

"Knoweth not love, knoweth not God.
John 4:8

Cassidy

"You have reached the Law Office of Grant Lebowski. No one is available to take your call. Please leave a message and you will be called within twenty-four hours. We value your business." Hearing the law office greeting, I lost my nerve and hung up. I have got to get my divorce papers filed and move out while Darius is in Africa which is just two weeks out, Cassidy thought while sitting in her BMW 750 outside their home. I really need to find a therapist as well because, if I don't get some anxiety medication, I might have a nervous breakdown. Looking at the exterior of our stately home, I was ashamed of how much I had put up with to maintain my lifestyle. Darius provided me things I had only dreamed about coming from a small town where we waited for the annual carnival to come to town for entertainment. I met Darius happenstance when he was in town for a meeting. Walking out of the library, I literally ran into him on the sidewalk. I dropped my purse because I was in such a hurry to feed my parking meter. Darius picked up my purse for me and apologized for being clumsy. I laughed and apologized as well. Hypnotized by his dazzling smile and handsome face, I stared at him in awe. He asked if he could see me again before he left town. We met that very evening for dinner. After he left, he visited me and courted me until we got married six months later. Our marriage was like heaven at first, then a new Darius emerged who was mean and cheated. Not wanting to lose the life I had become accustomed to, I put up with it all.

My parents told me this marriage wouldn't work out for "obvious" reasons. They cut me off shortly after I moved to Phoenix after marrying Darius. My sister will talk to me every now and then. They feel I embarrassed the family because I married a black man and had a bi-racial child. I thought my new financial status would impress them and lure them back into my life, but it didn't. I cried many a night feeling so hurt by their rejection, but I grew stronger. As my faith grew, I came to pity them because their ignorant racial views were beyond irrational. Somebody ought to study the biochemical origins of irrational, racist thinking. You have to know that something is wrong with you when you despise people you don't even know because of skin color. Still, I pray for the salvation of my family daily, but I also 'dusted myself off' and went on with my life because I couldn't make them change. Racists and other hateful people need to realize that their conduct has very real consequences for them. You cannot love God and hate other people. Either you "believe," or you don't.

That includes Darius because he didn't seem to feel there were consequences for treating people so badly. Still, I didn't feel I was on his level, so I willingly allowed him to denigrate and abuse me, but I was not going to tolerate him abusing our daughter, Arianna. This morning, I walked in on him berating her for wearing cornrows. That was the last straw. I had endured so much pain and humiliation in this marriage, but I will not let him rob our child of self-love and self esteem because he is ashamed of his culture. His twisted, self-hating views were actually lining up with my parents' immoral, repulsive mindset, which is ironic. About a year ago, Darius spewed venom at me for wearing my natural, curly hair to our weekly dinner date, as opposed to the straight and coiffed hairstyle that he and white people prefer.

After that, I knew I had to find out what else was eating at him, so I hired a private investigator to dig into his past. A lot of what he had told me about himself just didn't add up. For the sake of my child, I needed to know the truth.

After the search results were in, I found out that the story Darius had told me about his childhood had been a complete lie, although his education and professional background checked out. Once I found out he had a living mother and a sister, I knew I had to find them and paid the investigator more money to do just that. Afterwards, the private investigator told me that Joan, his mother, and Marilyn, his sister, lived together in Las Vegas. At the time, Marilyn was working as a slot attendant at a big casino and Joan was a peer counselor for a drug rehabilitation program. Emboldened by a glass of wine one evening, before Darius installed the cameras, I called their number and told them who I was. Marilyn answered the phone and didn't say anything for about twenty seconds before exploding with a loud scream. After that, I talked to Marilyn and Joan on 'Face Time' and we became family inside of an hour. Since then, we talk every few weeks, but I have not had the courage to tell Darius because I don't know what his reaction would be. Because of all the trouble he went through to keep his background a secret, I believe he would become enraged to find out I went digging and befriended his worst enemies, his own family members.

Lately, Marilyn has spoken of reaching out to him on her own and I have encouraged it. Darius has been particularly mean and short tempered for the past several months. When he does talk to me, it's about some Back-to-Africa program he's involved with but now wants to destroy. I guess, because I'm not black, he expected me to agree that anyone should be able to join the program to return to "their ancestral homeland," regardless of race. When I didn't, he blew a gasket and has been on a tear since then. If I'm honest though, it was not good between us even before that. He barely looks at me and rarely touches me. Our love life is non-existent. I know that he has cheated many times. When he's "involved," his pattern is always the same. "Honey, I'll be late tonight because of a new project," his alibi line of choice. He also dresses differently and wears certain pungent smelling cologne that he probably thinks smells primitive and sexy. During those times, he also treats me more formally and politely as though I'm stupid or something. I should have left many years ago, but I didn't have the strength to try and make it without him. I live like a queen, but have the self-regard of an abandoned pet. I don't want to become addicted to anxiety and pain pills because I have a child to finish raising, so I need to make some changes to save my own sanity.

I called Marilyn yesterday and am waiting for her to return my call. I need to tell her to go on and call him because he is changing daily for the worse. I don't bother Joan with it because she feels so guilty for hurting him that she won't act. Marilyn, however, was also a child when they were removed from their home, so Darius should not blame her for what happened in the past. No matter how upset or angry he may be, Darius has never unleashed on Arianna the way he did this morning. Also, he appears to be going to Africa without the knowledge of the others involved with the program which does not make any sense. If he is so against the program, why would he travel all the way to Africa in secret? I fear something is drastically wrong and I need Marilyn, who is very level-headed, to help me, help him. Even though I want out of this so-called marriage, I want my child's father to be mentally sound so that our child has two good parents. While he's in Africa, I will move out with Arianna and start my divorce proceeding, but I'm also going to try and get him some help.

CHAPTER 28

Karima

Two weeks out from the trip, I am stressed out inundated with all the remaining details related to our departure. The last board meeting before the pending trip to Africa will take place tomorrow by conference call. The main purpose of the meeting is to formally vote Darius out from the board and to nominate and vote in Keith Mackie in his place. Keith is the old high school friend who used to call me Queen. We are still in touch and are good family friends. There is no question that his politics and mindset are in line with the purpose of the program although he has mellowed with age like everybody else. Keith has a loving wife and two sons he adores. They live in Las Vegas, so meeting to handle program business will seldom be an issue.

Natu calls about twice a week. Our phone calls are getting more and more intimate. Both of us are super-anxious to see each other again. I wondered to myself how a fifty-five year old woman could get as excited about new love as a high schooler? I would have thought that age would dull the senses a bit and temper excitement, but they hadn't and that was the scary part. I had pictures of Natu I had taken with my cell phone. I printed and framed them, including a picture of the two of us I kept by bed. Hassan came over one evening, saw the picture and questioned me about him. I winded up telling him the whole story about Natu. I admitted I had strong feelings for him. Wise for his age, Hassan just smiled and hugged me saying, "It's about time." "I just hope you don't go moving over there, but I wouldn't even try to stop you if you did," he said. "Son, you know your Momma wouldn't leave you. I may wind up spending several months of the year over there, but I would stay here the rest of the time." After Hassan left that evening, I realized the conversation we had was one I didn't know I had been dreading. The closer I got to Natu, the more I understood that a long-distance relationship with him would be impossible. That man wanted me in his bed every night. We had discussed that we would need to figure out how to be physically together if we took the relationship further, but how could that happen if I also wanted to be near my family?

The next day, the Board met at 2:00 p.m. sharp. After formalities, I read the pertinent section of the by-laws and made a motion to remove Darius Jones from the Board of Directors for missing three consecutive meetings after due notice. The motion passed. The Directors also voted Keith Mackie in as the fifth Board Member and he accepted the position. Fatou prepared the minutes and placed them in the board binder. We finalized the plans regarding air confirmation numbers, stipends, budget reports and itineraries and adjourned the meeting. After the formality of ending the meeting, we chatted for a while and then said our goodbyes knowing that we would see each other at JFK in two weeks to the day.

That evening Skanki and I met for drinks. We hadn't seen each other or talked in several months, since right after I was fired from the job. Skanki nearly fell out of her chair when she saw the new me. "Karima, is that you," she asked? I said, "Stop playing Girl!" Skanki heaped accolades on me and boosted my ego big time. Skanki looked great herself, with her golden brown complexion, high cheekbones and green eyes, and I told her so. "You know I try to keep it together Karima. I have to stay ready," she declared.

Once our appetizers arrived, Skanki said, "I know you are super busy and about to go abroad again, but I'm grateful you took the time to get together with me because I really wanted to talk to you." I said, "You and I are soul sisters Skanki and I would never let you down." "Well, I'm just a little down because I was dumped recently by someone I really wanted to settle down with," Skanki said. "It's been about three weeks since I last saw Justin. I thought he would call and try to get back in, but he didn't. To my credit, I didn't call him either, but the whole thing got me to thinking if maybe I should consider your program for myself." I nearly choked once what she said hit me. I said, "Girl, you told me relocating to Africa was stoned tomfoolery." "I know, but look at me. I'm 49 years old with no man, no children and my family is on the East Coast. You are my closest friend and now you're a celebrity in the making traveling back and forth across the ocean. I've got nothing to stay here for. Plus, I want to change. My way isn't working. By the way, I want to be called Allison, from now on. My old nickname needs to die right along with my bad habits," Skan-, I mean, Allison, said.

I just looked at Allison and moved to her side of the table and gave her a big hug. In many ways, she was a victim of too much attention with her natural beauty and also because of the revealing way she dresses, but it wasn't a good time to get into all that. I said, "Allison, first of all, I am going to email you all the information for you to sign up for the program. The next group leaves in just over six months. But, more importantly, I am so happy for you for choosing yourself. The best advice I could give you is to get back into church where you can really acquire wisdom and re-set your standards. I can also tell you that once you rebuild your self-esteem based upon something that matters, which is your position as God's child, you won't allow yourself to be undervalued by another person again. Everything else will follow." Her reply was a big smile and a big hug for me. After that, our conversation took on a lighter note and we called it a night after the crème brulee, our favorite dessert.

CHAPTER 29

Karima

The next morning, I surveyed my custom designed closet for an outfit for church. The closet was a splurge gift to myself after I sold a home as a real estate agent. I had always felt that the closet was the best purchase of my life, besides my loft. I would never say that in front of "Clutch" though. I decided to wear a "sick" navy blue and brown plaid, double breasted suit with navy pumps and gold jewelry. Since the conclusion of my "come back" plan, I had decided I would not step foot out the door without being entirely put together. My mind wandered to Natu. Leaving for Senegal in just two days, the anticipation was torture. Last night, our conversation had become almost steamy. We are going to need to walk it back a bit when I get there to keep talk down. I could just hear it, "That American hoochie didn't waste any time snatching up one of our men." Laughing out loud at the thought, I also acknowledged to myself that I was concerned because I didn't want anyone to question my commitment to the program because of a new boyfriend. Deciding to discuss it with Natu in person once I got there, I continued to prepare for church.

Toweling off after a soothing bath, I started my daily routine of layering fragrances including body wash, body butter and perfume of the same brand, thereby extending the life of the fragrance throughout the day. Fully dressed, I called Hassan to make sure they were leaving on time. If they didn't, I wouldn't be able to save seats for the five of them. "Hello," said Hassan. "Good morning Son," I said. "Are you all leaving on time this morning?" "Ava fixed a big breakfast. The bacon got everybody up right away," he replied and continued. "You know Mom, I try to consecrate the house just like you did on Sunday mornings to set the tone for the Lord's special day. Ava fixes breakfast and I play gospel music and watch church services on television to usher in the spirit and to encourage reverence for the Lord in the girls." Fighting back tears, I realized that Hassan had never told me that before. "Son, I am so proud of you," I said. "Nothing, I mean nothing you could do in life is more important than being a man of God." We talked a few more minutes. "I am going to make all your favorites today Son, including Parmesan chicken, spaghetti, garlic bread, and ice cream cake. I'll meet you all after church at the house," I told him before we got off the line.

After we hung up, I pulled out my spring dinnerware and set my ten-piece dining room table, pared down to service for six. Hosting the monthly Sunday dinner had become a family tradition that made me deliriously happy. I thought, I'll put my new lavender stemware and purple hydrangeas on them today. Secretly, I had made each of my granddaughters promise me they would carry on the table setting and Sunday dinner tradition when they became adults. To my delight, they all agreed without hesitation and were starting to ride back to my home with me after church, instead of riding with their parents, to help prepare the table settings and place the serving dishes on the buffet.

CHAPTER 30

Karima

Arriving at the church at the same time, we piled into our usual pew and sat down. As expected, the message was on point and backed up by the Word. I noticed the girls making notes and looking up scripture during the sermon. After church, on our way to my home, the girls and I talked about the message and were astounded by how many times the word "love" appeared in the Bible. Madeline said, "It really makes me question how few disagreements we would all have if we just loved each other." "And, it's really stupid because we constantly need God to forgive us for our transgressions, but we don't want to forgive anyone else for theirs," Marie added. "I am so proud of you girls for making church a priority. Learning that word and making God number one in your life will bring about wisdom at a young age." Reaching our destination, we hauled out of the car.

Once Hassan and Ava arrived, all the food was set out on the Scandinavian, postmodern buffet. Ava led everyone in prayer before the meal saying, "Father, thank you for the provisions for the nourishment of our bodies. Thank you for the Holy Spirit guiding our thoughts and actions making us prioritize family. We ask for traveling mercy and for Karima's safety in Africa, all in the holy name of Jesus." "Amen," we all said in unison.

"Karima, I haven't been able to tell you this with all of us being so busy, but I am in total awe of you," said Ava. "You went from getting fired, to running a million dollar, non-profit corporation. How did you get the confidence to do such a thing?"

"You know, in some ways, I'm not sure myself," I said. "I just did some soul searching after they fired me and I knew it wasn't in me to get another dead end job. I just kind of felt like God is logical and wouldn't have given me all those great ideas to watch me to dismiss and ignore them. I just figured, let me settle on the best one and try and do it. God took it from there," I added. "But Glammie, how did you know people would want to go back to Africa," Lois asked. I sighed and said, "I didn't know for sure, but given how badly some of us have fared over here, what is there to lose?"

I told them, "I've been talking to one of our advisors over in Senegal who is planning a big, extravagant party for the people moving to Africa, a kind of welcome home party. She's not giving me a lot of detail, so the specifics will be a surprise to me as well. But the thing is, in all my life, I have never heard of a welcome home party for African American descendants of slaves returning to Africa. Although many have returned to Africa on their own, I have never heard of any sort of recognition, acknowledgement or publicity about Black Americans returning to Africa, so we have to celebrate our victories ourselves and control the narrative as they say. The idea that I had something to do with an event of this significance just makes me thank God for using me for his purpose." "Yep, it's a great feeling to be used by God," Hassan said.

Hassan and his family left around four that afternoon. After they left, I pulled out my most treasured bone china cup and saucer and enjoyed peppermint tea with honey. Laying back on the couch, it really hit me like a "Mack Truck" that my idea was actually changing lives, including mine. Not only that, but it could possibly be the catalyst for reconciliation regarding one of the most profoundly unjust human tragedies of all times. Talk about going full circle. From the unprecedented brilliance of Africans in Ancient Egypt, to centuries of chaos and discord leading to the scattering of Africans throughout the Americas and the Caribbean, never to return it seemed. All of the foregoing being ignored by history, leaving Blacks to cleave to their post slavery accomplishments, numb inside so disconnected from their ancestral homes and culture. If this program fulfilled its mission, it would be profoundly significant. A "W" for the underdog. I finished packing and relaxed while I could. Tomorrow, I will have to confirm all final details of travel for all the members. I would also need to confirm member completion of the online US based orientation and verify Visas for travel abroad. It would be a long day, but I wasn't the only one with a lot to do. Most of the relocators were anxious and had a lot of questions. For them, the program dedicated a live, toll free line with twenty-four hour availability to answer their questions and it was working out very well. On Tuesday morning, a bus in three major cities would take local travelers to their respective airports for the trip to JFK. It was ON. There would be no turning back.

PART FOUR

The Ultimate Reconciliation

CHAPTER 31

King and Queen

Too astounded to speak, Charles and Bridgette sat in the front, right seats of the mini-bus on the way to a hotel in Dakar, the largest city in Senegal. I cannot believe any of this really, Charles thought. For one, Bridgette and I will sleep in a bed together tonight, not on the ground in a tent. Hot dog! The itinerary gave all the "members," as we were now called, a free day to explore the city. Approaching Dakar from about three miles out, it certainly was not what I had expected because, from afar, it resembled any major city in America.

Dressed for her trip to the "Motherland", Bridgette wore a floor length, free flowing, forest green dress with bold, ethnic, earth toned jewelry and sturdy, leather walking sandals. I wore a navy dress shirt with jeans and Puma sneakers. We sat there together and took it all in. Compared to Phoenix, the landscape of West Africa looked like a forest. It was green with lush trees and plains for miles. The air was crisp and clean. There were cars from Japan, Europe and the States on both sides of the road, marking distance by kilometers, not miles. More unexpected were the unfamiliar cars that turned out to be designed, manufactured and sold by Africans for Africans, according to the tour guide. Never in my life had I heard that Africans were manufacturing and selling vehicles in Africa. I knew right then that we had a lot to learn about modern Africa.

Bridgette said, "Charles, I don't know about you, but I feel so good right now. Coming into that airport and seeing *us* in

131

charge in a real way has me feeling some kind of way. It's beyond the "chocolate city" dynamic in the States where a lot of us are working, but other people own the businesses and control the economy and the government. "Yeah, this is our first taste of being in the majority," Charles affirmed. The tour guide, a middle aged, bald man, began to speak into the intercom saying, "We want to welcome you all home. It is an honor that you have returned to the land of your forefathers. We will arrive at Hotel Jabar in about fifteen minutes. Please check in with guest services where you will get your room key. You will not be responsible for any charges for the room. It is 1:32 p.m. in our time zone. Today is a free day for you to explore the world-class city that is Dakar. We will meet again for breakfast at 8:00 a.m. in the hotel restaurant and, after a breakfast meeting, re-board this same bus, number seven, for the Village of Nafre where you will go through registration and then be given keys to your new homes. Again, welcome home. More information will be given to you at breakfast."

I smiled and rested my head on Charles' shoulder. It didn't seem real. Look at God, I thought. Then I revisited the thought in my head thinking, "Lord, why did I have to go through marriage, abuse, addiction and homelessness to find stability and happiness?" I was able to answer my own question when I recalled the church lesson that "we who are the called" recognize that it was the Lord who brought us through, not we ourselves. We are perfected through our struggles because we learn to trust in the Lord and not to "lean on our own understanding."

The bus pulled over and came to a stop in front of Hotel Jabar. The hotel exterior was quaint looking with a green and white awning hanging over the double entrance doors. There were window boxes under each of the plate glass windows on each side of the doors with bountiful flowers hanging down and showing off their vibrant colors. The interior had a "shabby chic" vibe, grounded by two identical brick colored sofas facing each other and covered with a variety of throw pillows of differing textures, shapes and colors.

Charles approached the reception area and was the first to check in. The registration agent was dressed classically professional wearing a sleeveless navy A-line dress accessorized with updated silver jewelry. She registered us and gave Charles the room key. Charles thanked the young lady, took the key and grabbed my hand. We took the elevator to the third floor. Uncharacteristically, we were relatively quiet with each other. Once we got into the room, we surveyed our surroundings and found them suitable, but we laughed at ourselves for being so prissy having just checked out of a homeless encampment. The furnishings were not brand new, but contained all the basics including a queen size bed, two chairs, two nightstands with lamps, a television, a remote control and a bathroom. We put our bags down and fell onto the bed. It was only the second time we had been together on an actual bed. Charles pulled me to him and we fell asleep.

"Wake up baby," Charles purred two hours later. Pulling myself out of deep sleep, I rubbed my eyes and pulled myself upright after I heard Charles speak. "Let's go eat and walk around," Charles said. We had been given the equivalent of forty dollars in Senegalese currency, the CFA franc. Dressing quickly, we left the room and headed outdoors.

A few hours later we returned exhausted with full bellies. "That was absolutely delicious. I never thought of eating flavorful stew inside a unique, sponge like bread. I think I'm going to like African food," Charles said. "I really enjoyed our little walking tour too. It was just as it would have been in any other major city except for so many people speaking French, something we may have to learn eventually." "I hope the things we picked up for our home will blend in well," I said. "Our home. I like the sound of that wifey," Charles crooned. We had gotten married before we left Phoenix to make sure we were "next of kin" since we would be living abroad. Charles proposed in our tent and placed a beautiful ring on my finger. I later found out it that he purchased it at Walmart with money his brother had wired him for the trip. It wasn't big, but it was beautiful and I adored it. I really didn't care how much he paid for it or where he got it from, it was a symbol of our love and commitment to each other and I was honored to be his wife. We were both still dumbfounded by the magnitude of the change in our lives, so we just relaxed and enjoyed the security of the private room.

After breakfast of French pastries, soft scrambled eggs and juice, we boarded the bus headed to Nafre. During breakfast, we got a few more pointers from the tour guide and, for the first time, found out that it would be possible to get jobs at either the expanded vineyard or at the new solar plant. That really got Charles' attention, since assembling or installing solar panels was a skill he could use anywhere in the world, he said. One of the things mentioned at the breakfast briefing was that the lives of the members moving to Africa would not change in the sense that they are free. Free to come and go as they please just as they would expect to do if they were born and raised here. We would not owe money to the program if we left and our homes were ours to hold on to and rent or sell if we decided not to stay. That came as a relief to Charles who planned to establish roots here and be able to visit his son in Arizona at least a few times a year. It was reassuring that the program leaders had the foresight to say those words to the members even though that was our understanding as well.

During the ride to Nafre, I told Charles, "I hope we have a bed in our home because you're a new man operating on a mattress if you know what I mean." Charles blushed and said, "Girl, you know how I do. You are my wife now and I believe a lot of things will change for the better." "I just cannot believe we are married and about to move into our first home together. Although our past life was just a day ago, it seems many moons behind us. We just seem to be different people. Regular people," I said. Charles retorted, "I know what you mean Bridgette. In my mind, already, I'm a different man. The thing I'm wondering about is how we will feel living here in Africa amongst "our people" who may not embrace us as the same as them. Maybe they will think of us as foreigners and not fellow Africans. On the other hand, assuming they do fully accept us, how might our psyches change not having to internalize daily discrimination, daily put downs, daily incidents evidencing bias against us in every arena because of our race?" I shook my head fully understanding the truth in his words.

Arriving in Nafre, we were all greeted by a welcoming committee of about eighty people. They seemed genuinely happy to meet us and to get to know us. We were led to a yellow stucco building, the Warma Building, where we signed program paperwork and received keys. They served us a lunch of sandwiches, chips, soda and cookies. After that, the welcoming committee staff people escorted each member to their new home. Our guide was named Fatima. She was friendly and talkative. She told us that she also lived in the new home community and offered to give us a tour of the village the next day and we accepted. Once we arrived at the front door of our beautiful, burnt orange, two-bedroom home, Fatima politely said her goodbyes. To my surprise, my husband picked me up and walked me over the threshold.

CHAPTER 32

Darius

I got off to a rough start leaving Phoenix because of flight delays which caused me to miss my connection in New York for Senegal. That meant I could not get to the village a day before the others arrived. In fact, I arrived after they were already here! That put a snag in my plan which was to get to the village, find their African counterparts and tell them about the people they had placed their trust in. I have some fake bank account statements, fake newspapers articles and fake criminal record searches to make them see they are dealing with crooks out to plunder their land and rape them for profit. I tried to obtain real documents, but I couldn't get them since I was not a signatory on the program accounts, not that real documents would have helped my cause. There was no question that the founders were legitimate although that makes no difference to me. Once I got to Senegal, I hired a driver named Hakim and made it to Nafre. He will stay the night here in Nafre through tomorrow or until my business is concluded for a handsome fee. If I'm able to make a love connection with Karima, I'll let him go and find another way back to the airport in Dakar where I have an open ticket to return to New York on "Air Afrique." Oui, oui!

So far, I have not made my presence known sitting in the back of Hakim's car with dark tinted window glass. I see they set up a welcome center. I saw a vast community of newly constructed homes when I approached the town which I had previously seen pictures of on their website. The usual suspects,

Karima, Kofi and Fatou mostly interacted with Africans who seemed to be the leaders from the local community. After an hour or so, the Americans were led to their new homes. Apparently, the Africans who got new homes had already moved in. I had to admit to myself that the African Americans appeared happy to be here from the looks on their faces. One small family cried together as they were led to their home. Whatever. The African leaders looked as if they were about to walk into a building. I needed to decide whether to approach the other American board members now or whether to wait for them to confront me after they are tossed out by the Africans. Then, I remembered Karima. If I piss her off right away, I won't even get a night with her while I'm here. I *need* to hit that at least once before I return to the States.

I was about to step out of the car when I saw a statuesque African man approach Karima. I watched as he literally swept her up in his arms and lifted her off her feet. They hugged each other very passionately and seemed elated to see each other, as though they were lovers. Incensed, I lost my cool and got out of the car and approached the group. Except for the African who hugged Karima, they all collectively gasped when they saw me. At that point, I had no plan because I impulsively left the car in a rage. The Africans who appeared to be walking away came back when they saw the reaction of the Americans to my presence. In a high pitched tone, Karima said, "What are you doing here Darius?" I replied, "What do you mean what am I doing here, I am a member of the Motherland Bound Board of Directors, aren't I? I have as much right to be here as anyone else." Karima replied, "Darius, we have not heard from you in months and you missed all the Board meetings since November, so you were voted off because you failed to meet the minimum requirements to maintain a seat on the Board."

At that point, I was about to have a meltdown. I was becoming so nervous and anxiety ridden. How could they have voted me out without telling me? I needed to reach my attorney friend Keith to find out if that is legal. To avoid looking weak though, I held my ground. I told them, "Even if you had proof of that, which I know you don't, I am here to expose all of you for who you are. Ladies, gentlemen, my name is Darius Jones and I am also a member of the Board of Directors of this program. I have some documents …" "Stop right there," said Kofi. "Have you lost your mind? How dare you come over here unannounced after disappearing for months with an agenda to try and destroy this program." Kofi pulled out his board binder and added, "Our corporate documents are right here confirming your removal from the Board for your information." I moved towards Kofi in a threatening manner and loudly proclaimed, "What are you afraid of Kofi. I am only here to inform my African brethren what is going on with you people. That's why I would like some time with the African leaders." Karima said, "I knew something was wrong with you months ago, but I didn't realize to what extent." I just glared at her trying to hide the sting of pain to hear her say that to me.

The one who hugged Karima stepped towards me and said, "I am one of the African leaders and we are not interested in anything you have to say. Don't you know that we have seen any and all documentation that we need to see about this program. Do you think we are a bunch of primitive, naïve dummies that would cooperate with a bogus foreign operation? We have defended and maintained our land from challengers for centuries. You obviously do not know who *we* are." Elder Whey added, "I know who you are Darius and it is your identity that is questionable. The Board has kept us informed about all developments on this program and we know when and why you were voted out. Any documents in your possession are likely inauthentic because *we* possess all genuine documents and have access to all other records involved with this program. You will not be given a private audience with us."

At that point, I snapped. I gave her "talk to the hand," as if to dismiss her dismissal of me and I got in the face of the one who hugged Karima. I said, "I don't know what your relationship is with Karima, but I suggest you keep your hands off her because I am also here to talk to her about a private matter. She is not an African woman, so please step aside so that I may speak with her privately." I noticed that Karima and everyone else inhaled and went speechless so I went on until the African reached for me but I was pulled back by Kofi. "Karima, may I speak with you for a minute," I pleaded as I backed away.

CHAPTER 33

Karima

I was experiencing one of the most euphoric, out-of-body feelings of happiness that I had ever felt in my life when I witnessed fifty African Americans receive keys to their brand new, mortgage free homes, nearly all of them for the very first time. How could an idea placed in my little head be the catalyst for such a feat? There were many Nafre residents there to greet us in addition to the welcome team. The welcome team's processing of the members was a thing to behold. Everything was so organized and streamlined. There was not even one mix up such as lost keys or anything that would have caused stress to the "children of the diaspora" who were returning to their ancestral homeland. Elder Whey and the Welcome Team could not have done a better job.

When Natu joined the group, we both completely forgot about trying to be appropriate and I just jumped into his arms. He was even more handsome than before. We were both so happy to see each other. I guess everyone will have to deal with it; we are obviously an item. All of us, the Elders, Fatou, Kofi and myself, were having a lovely time catching up and making plans for the next day when, of all people, Darius Jones got out of a car and confronted us. It took us a minute to grasp what was happening. He tried to get an audience with the Elders, but Elder Whey shut him down right away. He claimed he had documents to prove we were frauds, but he didn't know we had been working together too long and been too transparent for anyone on the Nafre team to even entertain his foolishness. Plus, they knew all about him including about the background check we did on him which revealed that, to a great extent, he had been living a lie as to his true childhood and background. We knew his educational and professional background credentials were authentic, but it turned out, he'd completely fabricated the story of his childhood, including lying that his mother and grandparents were dead, which was a sure sign of mental instability. Immediately after finding out he was living a double life, we were upset that we had a contrary spirit on our Board. Our mission is so vitally important and the mistake of having a divisive person in a powerful position could have derailed the whole project. But, as God would have it, Darius made some tactical errors, like not attending board meetings despite notice, so his removal was beyond reproach legally.

Back then, after we got over the initial shock regarding his misrepresentations about his background, we softened up and really felt badly for him since it was obvious he had not come to terms with his painful past. So, after he confronted us in Nafre and asked to speak to me privately, the Holy Spirit told me to speak to him. Natu was about to cold cock him, but I held his elbow in place when it went into that backwards motion before the fist found its target. I said, "I will speak to you privately Darius for just a few minutes, but before I do, we will go inside and look at your papers. Although I know you are here to try and destroy our program because we only accept descendants of Africa as members, you have sown a seed of doubt here today and I want our African counterparts to know for themselves that your papers are illegitimate. Chief Anuna said, "Karima, we don't need to see any papers, we know who you all are. The evidence of same has been shown to us for months." Referring to Darius, he said, "Young man, did you not see those new homes when you drove up today? Did you see the restoration of faith in the eyes of the people here today from your country? How can you, as a black man, not understand the purpose and the benefits of this program. I could have you removed from our land this very second, but if Karima is willing to speak to you, so be it." Before Darius could respond, Fatou said, "Chief, I agree with Karima that we should let this traitorous, misguided person show his documents so he cannot say that we did not consider his so-called evidence. We have nothing to fear."

With that, we re-entered the welcome reception area and sat at an empty rectangular table. Darius pulled out what looked like a bunch of Internet generated, pay search engine printouts. It was really wacky because the documents were clearly not reputable newspaper or magazine articles, or generated by banks, courts, or any other government authorities. None of the data matched our true legal names and the dates of birth didn't even correspond to our ages, by far. The so-called bank records were not bank records at all, merely rote numbers with the bank name on the top of each page. The team in Nafre already had our banking information due to numerous wires and payroll records. Darius had grossly underestimated the intelligence of the Elders to think he could come in with a stack of fake records and turn them against us. Natu said, "Karima, we have seen all we need to see here. Darius, please gather your paperwork and leave this village before sundown. Your driver has been given instructions to escort you to the international airport in Dakar." I stood up and asked a shocked Darius to follow me.

We sat on a bench not far from the building and I asked what he wanted to say to me. He said, "Are you involved with that African?" "That 'African' has a name, and even if I were involved with Natu, how is that your concern, Darius," I asked? "Karima, I'm going to be straight with you. You know that I want you. I was just playing with those papers to rattle you into taking me seriously. I knew I probably wouldn't be received well over here, but I had really hoped I could spend a few days with you and get to know you better. I lied to you in the restaurant when I said I wasn't flirting with you. The truth is, I've wanted you since I met you back in our school days when you were a young mother. I know I'm married, but that shouldn't stop us from being together. I can take care of you and I will." Completely dumbfounded, I was quiet for a minute as I tried to stay in my Christian character as opposed to cussing him out. The gall to propose an adulterous relationship so matter of factly, as though it made all the sense in the world. Finally, I said, "Look Darius, I would never involve myself with someone else's husband, so being together is absolutely not an option. I will be honest though and tell you that I was also attracted to you before I found out you were married, but since you clearly don't want to leave your wife, why don't you try and revive the love in your marriage? Also, I know you don't believe in what we are doing, so please, just walk away. Walk away and open your mind about why some African Americans want to be here. We are doing a lot of good. Please seek the counsel of the Lord and pursue peace. I wish you well," and I got up and walked away. He just glared at me with a crazed look in his eyes and walked to the waiting car and the driver drove him away.

CHAPTER 34

Anthony

I met Patrice, Clara and Aliyah, also members of the program, waiting to board the flight to Senegal at JFK. They were a pleasure to talk to and kick it with while we were waiting. When we got to Senegal and checked into Hotel Jabar, we agreed to meet at the front desk and find somewhere to eat at five. We didn't get too far in terms of sightseeing because it was getting late, but we found a bistro and had a nice meal together. We didn't really get into why we took such a drastic step as to move to Africa, but I sensed they had a story to tell. So did I for that matter. I figured that all of us relocating would get to know each other very well and stick together once we got settled in Nafre. That's not to say that we wouldn't bond with the local people, because we will, but coming from a common culture and experience, we are kindred souls who will understand one another.

Surveying Nafre after our arrival, it's so different than the big city life that I'm accustomed to. Even when I was in Europe, I played for and lived in big cities. Being very adaptable though, I feel like I can get used to it. After I decided to join the program, I started reading up on African history and read a lot of books on Senegal specifically. I found out it had been a French colony at one time, but Africans regained their independence in 1960. They have an abundance of natural resources, such as minerals, metals and vegetation indigenous to the area. Rice is grown here in abundance. I've always had an interest in farming and wondered if I could help the community make money from crops. I won't get ahead of myself though and start assuming the local people don't already have all that going on. I'll keep my thoughts to myself until I know what's up.

My welcome committee guide, Pa Goffi, escorted me to my one bedroom home. The exterior was painted gray and it had curb appeal. I went inside and discovered it had a great layout including an area where I can set up a small office. A lot of money has passed through my hands, but I have never owned a home. I feel very proud of myself because of this home even if I didn't pay for it myself. Having the office space is very important to me because I still plan to play my video games such as "2K" through the Internet, so my life won't change that much. I like that Dakar is so close to Nafre so I can go to the big city anytime I want to or get to the airport without much fanfare when I visit the States. I unpacked and called my people and let them know I was settled in. I set up my "Play Station" and played some games with the same guys I usually play with.

I find myself thinking about the police out here too. I know they won't racially profile me for being black, but I hope they won't be giving a 'brotha the side eye for coming from the States. I guess I brought my fears and paranoia with me even though I'm now a member of the majority. I had to laugh at myself. I decided to keep up with the progress of the NBA African league, but to put that whole thing on the back burner for now. I really want to give Africa a chance to become my home, for real, and maybe even start a family. There weren't many single people traveling with the program, so I'll have to make an effort to build a local family around me. There was a Senegalese woman named Fatima that caught my attention. She was part of the welcome team. I'm going to keep my eye on her.

CHAPTER 35

Natu

Karima is one beautiful woman. I feel so lucky that she has chosen to keep company with me. Seeing her again nearly took my breath away, but our reunion was interrupted. I thought I might be going to jail for assaulting that Darius person for a minute. I knew he was interested in Karima before he even asked to speak to her privately. I could feel it because of how he was staring at me. He jumped out of that car right after I took her into my arms for the first time since her arrival in Nafre. I conjured up a wealth of restraint in allowing that conversation to take place between them, but I was not going to dictate to her and have Karima thinking I was some kind of a controlling buffoon.

Once she returned, she told us what he said. It was a serious matter so I didn't want to reduce it by laughing at his ludicrous proposition, but it was funny. He must be obsessed with Karima to fly over here to try to start a romance with her. He must also be crazy to think he was going to have a good time with her after trying to destroy her dream. Not just her dream, but the dream of everyone benefitting from the program. Absolutely delusional. The more I thought about it, I realized he may actually be dangerous and he is still in Senegal. The driver would drop him off somewhere and Darius would be free to try and devise another deranged plan to get at Karima or to hurt the program. I pulled Kofi to the side and told him I would try to get a tail put on him so that we might know his whereabouts and comings and goings. I planned to stay vigilant as well.

Karima, Kofi and Fatou plan to stay at "Victoria's" again for their two week stay. After our group discussion about Darius, Karima and I were overdue for some alone time so we decided to go to my new home, which would also be the first time she would see the interior of one of the homes. She cried in my arms after touring my residence and the immediate area. I guess I can understand how she must have felt at seeing her dream materialize and become something you could see and touch. And not any old dream, but a dream that symbolically reunited lost and separated countrymen. We talked about it though and agreed that you can't get too caught up in the sense that God is the ultimate maestro. He works through all of us for the fulfillment of *his* plan. When you feel like he actually used you, you just have to be humble and avoid getting puffed up and be grateful he *could* use you for his purpose, although he can use anybody, good or bad.

Once we sat down and settled into my new den, I showed her my divorce decree. I said, "The settlement was fair to both sides and we both moved on I suppose. I'm just glad we got it done after our children became adults. It's funny though, now my ex is asking questions about me because she knows I'm a big part of this project, which is the talk of the country. It's as though she has regrets now that I'm "successful." That Mike Jones song came to my mind and I sang, "Back then, they didn't want me, now I'm hot, they all on me. I said…" Karima fell out laughing. Yeah, we played that one over here too, I told her.

I filled Karima in on the last few months regarding the ordering and building. I told her about all our construction staff and the Senegalese residents of the new homes. She told me about the tasks they completed in the States to get us to this point. While we were talking, the Motherland Bound program was mentioned on the news because the group had arrived and moved into their homes. By then, our nervousness had dissipated. I pulled her to me and kissed her for the first time. It was a gentle, exploratory kiss. As we got comfortable, the passion took over rendering both of us breathless. The kiss confirmed what I already knew. This was one of those relationships with chemistry, which either you have or you don't. Over the phone, Karima had told me that she hadn't been involved with anyone for many years. I understood and respected her reasons for shunning romance. She's such a beautiful woman, inside and out, but it was still hard to understand how American men would not relentlessly try and break her resolve, not including Darius. In the end, I'm the recipient of their lack of judgment or tenacity.

Our kiss grew in intensity. She may have been out of the game for a while, but she was passionate and the need we had for each other was greedy and urgent. Her natural and tender touches weaved her into the folds of my heart. There was no need for conversation, our bodies did all the talking as we touched, explored and kissed each other's faces and necks. I decided not to initiate anything more than that so as not to scare her with too much, too soon. I almost felt dirty even thinking of trying to become one with a virtuous woman like Karima until she is my wife. But something between us had been solidified. From that point forward, she was my woman and I planned to treat her as such.

Exhausted from travel and non-stop activity, we fell asleep in each other's arms. When she awoke, Karima asked me to take her to Victoria's to check in because nightfall was approaching and she didn't want to lose her reservation. I cut on my porch light and we headed to the shoreline where Victoria's was located.

CHAPTER 36

Karima and Natu

After I checked in at Victoria's, I asked Natu to follow me to my room which was more like a little villa, ideal for privacy. Since we would be staying for a couple of weeks this time, we opted for the villas as opposed to the single rooms. Now that I have Natu in my life, I had to consider the ramifications of my comings and goings. Africans are more conservative than Americans, I believe. I really didn't want local people to view me the wrong way for "entertaining" a local man who is not my husband. It would also appear we had just met each other, which was even worse. Even so, we are dating, so I was not going to act like a teenager and kiss him on the cheek and say goodnight at the door just because someone might see him enter my room. Having Natu in my room briefly was not a real problem anyway because I wasn't going to let things go too far, too fast, which was almost always a mistake. No matter how much we had talked on the phone long distance, we still needed to get to know each other as people and in person before becoming fully involved. But, right now, at this minute, I didn't want to be apart from him, so he came inside. We had waited so long to see each other again and I felt so comfortable with him.

After we entered the room, Natu inspected it for safety reasons and then took me into his arms. He kissed me again and it was so special. We were full of desire. I managed to say, "Natu, if we keep on like this, we're going to get to the point of no return." "You're right baby, and I understand," he said. "Wherever we go in Nafre, it will pretty much be close quarters and I'm not going to do anything to spoil your good reputation as the founder of this great endeavor." He continued, "It's still early though, so how about we go to dinner now and I'll drop you off afterwards once I know your room is safe." Natu thought, "I didn't tell her that I was afraid Darius might still be lurking somewhere in the area." The tail on him was going to be fruitless until they spot him for the first time since he left before we called for help. Natu recalled when he was enamored with Karima months ago and watched her from his balcony one evening, just wishing and wanting to make her his. So, in a crazy way, he could relate to Darius. Karima was the kind of woman that got under your skin, deep.

Natu and I went to the same local restaurant we dined at in the Fall and had a great evening. We both ordered broiled fish with lemon, butter and capers with cassava. We danced and enjoyed the local wine before going back to the hotel. Once we returned to Victoria's, at Natu's request, we called Fatou and Kofi and asked to stop by their room briefly. It turned out their villa was only two doors down from mine, which made me feel safer. The men talked as Fatou and I de-briefed the day. I overheard Natu speak to Kofi about efforts to confirm the whereabouts of Darius in case he decided to stay in the area looking for me. That made me a little nervous, but I appreciated the men thinking cautiously on my behalf. Natu and I headed over to my room and he came in, checked out it, gave me a passionate good night kiss and left for home. After my shower, I got straight into bed to be fully rested for the first day of orientation tomorrow. Before I fell asleep, I thought about Natu and what his expectations might be regarding intimacy between us. Although I had told him that I remained uninvolved with men for many years as I raised my son, I never told him that I had only been intimate one time in my life, which was the time my son was conceived. As much as I wanted to be with Natu, in my heart of hearts, I wanted him for the long, long run, not just a part time boyfriend. Also, my devotion to the Lord made me feel like, I've been celibate this long, I may as well give the gift of my whole self to my husband rather than to a boyfriend living on another continent. Growing sleepy, I was dozing off, but not before I resolved to hold off physical relations with anyone until I got married. Hopefully, the handsome and virile Natu Bello would become my husband.

CHAPTER 37

Patrice, Clara and Aliyah

Spread out on their u-shaped sectional, each of them, Patrice, Clara and Aliyah claimed their spot on the couch with long-term intentions in their minds. The television was mounted to the wall in the exact right spot. Still full from lunch, they channel surfed trying to become familiar with local offerings. No where near the five hundred plus channels they were used to, but there were entertaining nature shows, cooking channels, local news and sports. All black news anchors and storylines were completely new and entirely refreshing. "Look, I found a movie channel which features Nollywood and Ghanian films," said Patrice. "What is Nollywood?" asked Clara. Patrice told her about the motion pictures made and filmed in Nigeria and beyond. "Most of them are quite good, whether big or small budget films," Patrice told her. "Maybe we can start something akin to a movie theatre here featuring the great Nollywood films a few times a week." "You may have something there, Patrice," said Clara. "That would be a great way for the residents to all get to know each other. Remember that lady Fatima who was in charge? The lady we got our keys from? We could ask her whether there is a place big enough to hold about a hundred of us and a big screen," Clara added. "We could also think up some other activities for networking and bonding 'cause we 'gon put Nafre on the map!", Patrice screamed while high fiving Aliyah.

Each lost in their own thoughts, Patrice relived it all in her mind. Leaving the house. Waiting in the airport. Seeing all the other hopeful, black people relocating through the program. Meeting some of them, including Anthony Wright. Hotel Jabar. The ride to Nafre. The big welcome. The house. Unreal.

I hope I don't find a way to mess this up, Patrice thought. Everyone seems so clean and genuine, but sometimes I feel dirty and unworthy. I'm thankful to be over here in such a new and unfamiliar environment where I don't know anyone. I can just spend my mental energy learning this culture instead of being haunted by my past. If I weren't in this unique situation, I might have craved drugs again one day or have become triggered by something or someone in Baltimore, so this is a double blessing. No one knows my past out here and I don't intend to share it either. If the managers do somehow know, they would not disclose it. I am sure of that. These people remind me of my angel, Sister Daly. I could just tell God was in her. First thing tomorrow, I am going to find out where the local church is so that I can arrange to be baptized on this soil. I know that God forgives me, but I need help to forgive myself. I want to feel clean and as pure as snow in God's eyes and to never again look back in self-judgment.

The next morning, we went through the welcome basket and found all kinds of basic necessities, including many American food staples. The refrigerator already contained eggs, milk, juice and butter. We all fell out when Mom said, "That welcome team ain't no joke!" We were able to cook a breakfast of pancakes and juice. During breakfast, we made a grocery list and then got ready for the day.

CHAPTER 38

Anthony

I decided to go outside and look around, and who did I see? Fatima. She was with a couple who I believe are from Phoenix. They saw me and waved me over. I closed my door and joined them. "Hi, I'm Fatima Chebo. This is Charles and Bridgette King from Phoenix. I'm about to give them a tour of the area. Would you like to join us?" "Of course," I said, disbelieving my good luck. "I'm Anthony Wright from Atlanta. You know, I met a family from Baltimore who probably would want to join us. Do you mind if I knock on their door?" "Not at all, we'll wait," said Fatima. Anthony returned a few minutes later with Patrice, Clara and Aliyah. Fatima recognized them from the welcome reception. Introductions were made and we all started walking.

Fatima told us a little bit about the village of Nafre. She said, "After Senegal's independence from France was secured in 1960, this area was inhabited by about ten families and it grew from generation to generation. Our main source of commerce is agriculture. We developed rice farms, vegetable farms and planted grape vines decades ago, which we still harvest. We export almost everything we produce. The only problem is the relatively small scale of the production." That answers my question, I thought. Maybe I can be a part of helping them increase production?

Walking through the new home community, Fatima took us to the park and to the community center, which included computer stations, gym equipment and a kitchenette. The park had a few swings and a small water feature for toddlers. Fatima reminded everyone that the orientation would start that afternoon and go on for one business week. After that, on March 29th, there would be a big welcome home celebration for them. Fatima held back on the scale of the celebration though. As the primary planner, Fatima wanted as much of it as possible to be a surprise. She thought to herself, "They have no idea that dignitaries and celebrities from America and West Africa would be in attendance."

As we left the home community and walked towards the village, I asked Fatima if she lived in the complex. She nodded affirmatively and said, "I live on your street Anthony." "How many bedrooms do you have," I asked, trying to figure out if anyone lived with her. She told me, "One." Fatima was surprised by my questions, I could tell. But what Anthony didn't know was that Fatima was happy to engage with the tall, handsome 'brotha from the States. Fatima asked me, "Anthony, you are so tall. Are you a basketball player?" "I played professionally in Serbia for a few years until I got injured. I hope to play again one day," I responded, deciding to keep my hopes and dreams to play in Africa to myself. Fatima was even more beautiful close up I observed. She wore her shoulder length hair in a fluffy ponytail and sported medium size, gold hopes reminding me of "Sade," another African queen. She came off very high fashion, wearing tight jeans and a white linen shirt, a little out of place in Nafre. Her eyes were brown, which complimented her even, cinnamon skin color. She was about five feet, ten inches, which was a nice height from my perspective as a potential love interest for me. The other people in the group had stopped talking and just listened to us, obviously wondering if love was in the air.

The village was really one main street with about ten buildings on each side. It was obvious that some of the buildings contained restaurants and other businesses, but there was little to no signage. The other buildings looked habitable, but were empty. Accustomed to multitudes of commence at every turn, the members got silent and their faces showed concern which

Fatima picked up on. She said, "I know this is very different from America, because I have been there. Once you get used to a slower pace of life, it won't bother you and you can always go to Dakar when you crave the big city. I'm personally hoping that all of us can work together and use these buildings and start businesses for ourselves. Rent is very cheap here and we need everything. With all the new residents and the recent attention Nafre is getting, there should be enough support for new businesses. This program has the people of Nafre ready to join forces with you to update and improve our village. Just think, whatever dreams and talents you have can be realized here in Nafre. We just have to be creative and courageous." Clara responded, "Fatima, that is music to my ears. I play the piano and I have always wanted to give lessons. Patrice here has wanted to open a full service salon. This could be our opportunity to get both dreams off the ground." Bridgette said, "I love to juice and make smoothies. If I could open that kind of business, I would do twenty flips while chewing bubble gum!" We all laughed at the thought of it. "This is all so amazing. Truly a dream come true," Charles said.

Clara asked where the nearest food market was and Fatima pointed it out. The market wasn't much bigger than a "bodega" corner store, but it had all the basics until they could get to a larger market in Gambia or Dakar, according to Fatima. Fatima also pointed out that the open air market was available each weekend where fruits, vegetables, chicken and seafood could be purchased. "How would we buy cars out here," I asked. "Unless someone in town is selling one, you can get one in Dakar," Fatima responded, and then added, "I can help you with that." "Thanks much," I replied ecstatically. I'll use any reason to spend some private time with her I thought.

CHAPTER 39

Darius

Luckily, Hakim brought me to the exact place I needed to be, Victoria's. The "powers that be," that African and Kofi, had "instructed" Hakim to take me straight to Dakar. As if. Hakim was trying to do as he was told heading straight for Dakar, acting like a scared little schoolgirl. I said, "Fool, don't you know I'm the one paying you!" I told him to drop me off at the best hotel in the area and he dropped me at Victoria's. I had just walked out of the lobby with my room key in hand when I heard Kofi's voice. I quickly slipped around the corner and saw him and Fatou check in. I knew Karima wouldn't be far behind them.

I tarried on to my room and spied from my balcony spotting Kofi and Fatou going into a room not far from mine. If they thought they could humiliate me and cast me off like a jilted bride, they had another thing coming. Once I figure out how to get some food into my room and get some sleep, I will confirm their room numbers for starters. I hadn't planned to bring my "piece" over here, but I'm so glad I went on and packed it, because now I need it.

CHAPTER 40

Karima

The orientation, to take place over a week, will start this afternoon. This morning, the founders, Elders and welcome team leaders will meet and finalize all details of the agenda. The plan is to divide each day into two segments, morning and afternoon. Each morning, the members will learn everything about prevailing law, law enforcement, local customs, village culture and Senegalese culture as a whole. In the afternoons, there will be less structure and all the villagers, new and old, will simply talk and get to know each other. To keep them focused though, they will be tasked with planning and calendaring social activities for all village residents, two per week, to promote morale and bonding of all Nafre residents. On the last day of orientation, all members will receive legal forms and instructions on starting businesses in Nafre. Last but not least, at the end of that last day, each homeowner will receive their deed of trust, better known as the title to their home!

Elder Whey had told me during one of our long-distance conversations before I got here that the Elders were hoping this program would encourage more businesses and opportunities in the area. She said that the time of everybody just living off the land had passed. From my last trip here, I knew for a fact that Nafre residents had the ideas and the skills to run a variety of small businesses, but they needed motivation and incentive. Elder Whey figured the African Americans would likely be more entrepreneurial minded than the Nafre residents, but that the locals would soon join in not wanting to be outdone and overcome by the new residents. That's why the business incubator concept would be introduced on the last day of orientation to get things moving beyond the dream stage.

Once we organizers received and understood our assignments for orientation, the tables and chairs were arranged for ease of conversation in anticipation of the expected large group of members. Day One of the orientation was set to begin at 1:30 p.m. promptly.

CHAPTER 41

Darius

After a great meal of broiled fish, potatoes and salad from room service, I relaxed. Feeling pretty good about my PI skills, I laid down with my hands behind my head on this my second day in Africa and pondered my next move. Fortunately for both of them, I saw that African leave Karima's room shortly after he had entered last night. If I even *thought* they were in there throwing down, there would have been hell to pay. As much as I want to punish all of them for dressing me down in front of all those people, more than anything, I want Karima to give me a chance, especially now that it's confirmed that she was feeling a brother at one time. But if I can't have her, I don't think I can bear to know someone else is with her. I had to face it, I was sprung like a chicken. When she reached out to me about joining the Board, I knew our relationship was meant to be. I'm not trying to catch a case over here though, so I've got to find a way to make her see that she belongs with me before we leave.

My ring tone for home sounded off and I thought, "What the hell could she want calling me knowing I'm over here?" "What's going on Cassidy?" I asked sharply. "Hey Darius, I'm sorry to call you when you're so far away, but I wanted to tell you something very important and it couldn't wait," she said. I responded, "Well, what is it?" "Two women called here wanting to speak to you. They said they were your sister and your mother. They want to see you," said Cassidy. Stupefied, I grew faint, fell down and
dropped the phone.

Knocked down by the weight of her words, I stayed down for a few seconds until I heard Cassidy screaming my name and saying "hello, hello." I grabbed the phone off the bed and with as much bass in my voice that I could find, I said, "Yeah Cassidy." She was asking me a bunch of questions out of concern. I assured her that I was okay, but I didn't answer any of her questions about her revelation and she grew more and more upset by that. "There's something else I need to tell you Darius," she said. I didn't like her tone and dreaded more bad news, but I stayed in character waiting for her to speak. With hesitation in her voice, she said, "I'm leaving you Darius. Arianna and I have moved out." Unable to believe what I just heard and still reeling from her earlier news, I had no words. I hung up in her face.

I pulled out the cognac from the wet bar and drank it straight out of the bottle. I felt weak and dizzy, so I laid down on the bed. My head was spinning. My whole world had just collapsed and I was thousands of miles from home, chasing a piece of tail and trying to control a group of people who didn't even respect me.

My mind wandered back to Karima. Even if she didn't want me, she was a warm, sweet person. I wanted to be comforted by her in my time of need. I wanted her to hold me in her arms, kiss me on my face and tell me it would be alright.

But it would never be alright. My past had found me. I felt so ashamed. I should have looked for them and been the man in our family. I've been in the financial position to find them for years, but I considered my mother dead and I let the fear of being exposed keep me from looking for my beloved sister, Marilyn. They, on the other hand, loved me enough to look for me and found me. Damn.

Cassidy has left me and taken my child. Not going to happen. Cassidy can leave if she wants to, but the child stays with me. I will get the best family attorney in Phoenix to make sure she gets exactly what she came into this marriage with, nothing! After all I did for her and this is what I get. And, she pulls this stunt while

I'm on another continent. That ratchet, ungrateful female is going to get what's coming to her. I knew a year into the marriage I had made a mistake, but she got pregnant so I honored my vows. Truthfully, I don't even know why I pursued her and married her so quickly.

Jumping up, I decided that I had to get out of Senegal and handle my business. I pulled up the cameras in and around my home in Phoenix on my cell phone. That wench had cleaned everything out except for my private quarters. I fell down and cried. I cried, but my tears didn't lessen the rage that boiled in me.

I should be able to catch that "red eye" flight to London tonight and connect to New York from there. But, before I go, Karima is going to understand the depth of my feelings for her. She is going to feel every inch of me. Right now, those 'goodie two shoes' are in an orientation session. When Karima returns to her room, I will be waiting for her to make love to her and then I will take her back with me. If that African enters her room, he will regret it.

CHAPTER 42

Fatima

"On behalf of the welcome committee of Motherland Bound, I want to welcome each of you again to Nafre and to the first day of Orientation. Those of you from America have managed to become a part of world history by returning to your ancestral homeland through a program designed to elevate the lives of everyone involved with it," I announced. "Thanks to everyone for signing the releases as the entire orientation will be videotaped for training purposes," I added. "We have a few speakers before we get started on our agenda for this afternoon. First and foremost, the brainchild and founder of this organization, Karima Powers, will address you. Karima is the living embodiment of what it means to have faith and to take action regarding your hopes and dreams. God placed a vision into her soul and she had the courage to go after it. As a result, we are all sitting here receiving keys to new homes and many us are also about to open the businesses of *our* dreams. What is happening here is so powerful, that it's almost scary. With no further ado, Karima Powers," I shrieked.

"Good afternoon everyone," Karima said. "I want to thank each of you, everyone in this room, for being here and for participating in this program. I will just speak from the heart because I am among family. Being honest, I am completely flabbergasted by what has happened in such a short amount of time. Never underestimate the value of the pressing matters of your soul. For me, it was a strong desire to do something to uplift the condition of my people. My dreams in that regard were so outlandish, this one included, that I started thinking I was crazy. The ideas I came up with, as a poor woman, were so large in scale that only God himself could have pulled them off. Only God. Look at God! Look at what the seed he planted in me brought about. That little mustard seed is changing the course of history. My friends, Fatou and Kofi Diallo, embraced my dream, financed it and accepted it as a part of their destiny. Let us make this a success. Let's stay as positive as we are today. Let's be patient with each other. Let's embrace each other as family, because we are. Let's remind the world of who we are. Let not our ancestors have died and suffered in vain. Today, this afternoon, let's just talk. I would like for each person to tell us who you are, that's all. Tomorrow, we will get into the meat of our agenda. Thank you Brothers and Sisters."

Karima's speech was short, but powerful. Everyone in attendance clapped thunderously and were clearly moved. I know I was. Now that the founders and the members from the states are here, I am learning so much more about the program. I mean I thought it had an outstanding premise from when I first heard about it, but I am in awe of it now. Many of the residents met for the first time today since this was the first event where all the homeowners were in attendance, including the historical Nafre residents. After the meeting, many of the residents, new and old, stayed on and talked. I could see the bonding taking place. We are onto something here. Nafre is going to be changed for the better I was sure of it.

The "Welcome Home" event is less than two weeks out. The stage has been constructed and the speakers and sound system components will be installed two nights before the event and tested extensively until the actual event. Reservations for all speakers and guests have been confirmed at "Queen Candace Hotel" in Dakar for the night before the ceremony. Since the event starts at 4:00 p.m., they will have plenty of time to get to Nafre before the event since the ride is just over two hours. All of the

African American, Motherland Bound members, who are the real guests of honor, will sit on lifted rectangular tables, about two feet below the stage. The tables will be covered in gold leaf paper and other metallic components and will be dressed and decorated to a degree fit for royalty. The lifting of the tables ensures that those being honored will be visible to the large crowd of attendees who will be sitting below them on the ground level. At some point, the returning descendants of Africans will be ushered to the stage where they will be adorned with a traditional robe, with all the majestic design details, which will be theirs to keep. The program will include speakers, dancers, video presentations, food, music and traditional entertainment. If I have my way, this event will be talked about all over the world.

CHAPTER 43

Natu

Towards the end of the first day of orientation, I motioned for Kofi to join me outside. "Man, that Darius is probably still in our midst. The police located his driver, Hakim, who told him he left Darius somewhere near Nafre at Darius' insistence. He claimed that he didn't leave him at any specific location, just on the side of the road about a mile out of town." Kofi sighed and said, "This is a nightmare. We're out here making history and what not and this idiot is trying to ruin everything. We have to be very careful because he might even have a gun since he could easily have packed one in his checked bags." "Well, I'll make it my business to get mine right away and keep it on me in case it's needed," I responded. "You know, there's an excellent chance he is staying at Victoria's as well since it's the only hotel close to American standards in the area. He probably just rested up last night, but I think we should plan on him making a move this evening. Can you get some back up for us," Kofi asked me. "For sure. I agree with you. He probably won't try and stay in the area long, so this may be the ideal time for him to strike. My guess is that he will try and get at Karima some kind of way." Seeing the logic in my words, Kofi responded, "I couldn't agree with you more." "Okay, so you get Karima to her room Kofi, and I'll go home, get my gun and make the arrangements for back up and then drive back over to Victoria's as soon as I can get it all done," I said. Kofi nodded in agreement.

Once the first day of the orientation was in the books, the Elders, Board members and I met in the same room to de-brief. With heavy hearts, Kofi and I told everyone what was going on. Elder Tamu said, "You see, this is just what I was talking about at that first meeting. We don't want people coming over here with guns and bringing violence to our door." Karima just hung her head. She could not believe such a thing was happening in the midst of so much good. Kofi addressed the group and said, "I am so sorry and so disappointed myself that a sick, broken spirit would travel all the way here to try and stop God from acting, but that is precisely why he will fail and we must press on, unafraid. At the end of the day, Darius is not strong enough to stop what we have started." Karima said, "Elder Tamu, from the very depth of my soul, I apologize for this mess, but I believe that it will end tonight. We will be ready for him and will put him on a plane to a location off this continent. Please, let's hold hands and pray for deliverance from this sick individual."

I felt so badly that Karima had to deal with this. We bowed our heads and I led them in a prayer for God's covering and deliverance of the mission of the program.

After which I whispered in Kofi's ear, "Buy me some time."

CHAPTER 44

Karima

What a day! Natu told me that he needed to go home to pick something up and then he would meet me at the hotel. I am exhausted and plan to shower, change and rest for a bit before Natu gets there. As I rode back to Victoria's with Fatou and Kofi, Fatou reminisced on the day. "I'm telling you, in just one day's time, the countenance of the members has changed. Remember Patrice, the single mother? Yesterday, at the airport, although I saw hope in her eyes, she still presented with the appearance of defeat. I know from her disclosures that she's been through a lot in her life. Today though, she shined like a pageant queen, introducing her family to people, asking questions and she smiled so much. "I noticed that too," I said. Kofi, recalling the family atmosphere in the room said, "We have all worked hard to make it to this day, but I feel like the members picked up the baton today. They will be the ones to dictate the end game to our story. If they manage to co-exist peacefully and build their economy with the push-start we gave them, they will make us all proud and I believe they will." He added, "And much respect to you Karima for your introductory greeting. It was short and from the heart, but epic in the sense that it illuminated the low odds of something like this ever happening." Pleased that he got the main point I was trying to convey, I said, "That's why I had to give credit where credit is due. Only the Lord could have allowed this miracle to take shape."

"Before we go to our rooms ladies, let me buy you a congratulatory drink at the pool bar" said Kofi, as we walked into the luxurious lobby at Victoria's. Fatou and I readily agreed and we all walked through reception to the pool area to enjoy some delicious, tropical drinks and continue discussing the day.

After we left the pool bar, Kofi and Fatou walked me to my door, but didn't come in. We were all so very tired. I walked in and, as the door closed, someone's hand covered my mouth and pulled me into the room! I tried to scream but I couldn't because the grip on my mouth was very strong. I was pulled towards the bed backwards and then I saw that I was being held by Darius! He sat on the bed and pulled me onto his lap such that we were both facing the door. Even though he held me in place with his strength, he was panting and started kissing my arms and face as though we were in a romantic moment. He caught his breath and started to speak as I struggled to get away from him. Lovingly, he said, "Karima, sweetheart, you smell so good and your luscious mouth smells of coconut. Don't resist me. I don't want to hurt you. We've got to leave, but I want to make love to you before we go so that you will know you belong with me. I have wanted you for so long. Please don't continue to resist me. I know you want me the same way I want you and I appreciate you being honest with me yesterday." It was a full case of reality distortion. He started pulling down my pants and also tried pulling his down with his free hand. I bit his finger and he snatched it back and replaced his hand over my mouth again, this time with more brutality and force. I tried to yell out, but I couldn't make a sound. I was no match for him physically. With his other hand, he was still working my pants down and, sitting on his lap, I was clear about his condition and about his intentions.

I didn't expect Natu to get to the hotel for a while and Kofi and Fatou thought I was safely locked in my room, so even though I was terrified, I had to figure out how to prevent being sexually assaulted by this animal. In a panic state, I struggled to think straight. I decided to stop resisting hoping he might ease up so that I could pretend to go along with his plan long enough to get out a scream and run. Seconds after I stopped fighting him, he eased his hand from my mouth but, rather than allow me to breathe, he covered my mouth with his and tried to kiss me, but I quickly shook myself away and jumped up from his lap. I started screaming before he caught me again. I heard a loud thump and the door flew open! Natu, Kofi and a local policeman stormed in! I fell to my knees and cried.

Before I knew what was happening, Darius snatched me up and pointed his gun at the other men. Holding me in front of his chest, he was using me as a shield and a hostage! Both the officer and Natu pointed guns at Darius as well. Darius said, while grabbing his bag, "You don't want none of this. Karima is leaving with me. Move out of the room slowly or somebody is going to take a bullet. She is my woman and we are returning to the States together. Get your ID and passport, baby," he ordered. His gun was pointed at them though. Genius Darius had a gun in one hand and the other hand around my waist, but my hands were free. Natu kept looking hard at me, then at my right arm over and over and I finally got the signal. I abruptly lifted my right arm forcing the gun out of his hand and it fell to the ground. Darius inadvertently let me go and tried to retrieve the gun, but it was too late, the men pounced on him and the officer was able to put him in handcuffs. It was over.

CHAPTER 45

Kofi and Fatou

"Something told me to go into her room and check it out before allowing her to go in, but I didn't want her to feel I was being intrusive, so I ignored my gut instinct and look what happened," said Kofi. "You mean, what almost happened honey. Let's remember that you and the other men saved Karima's life. That lunchbox Darius had a gun," Fatou reminded him. "Plus, by your taking us to the pool bar, Darius didn't have time to execute on his sick plans for Karima."

I realized that Fatou had a point. I needed to stop beating myself up and be thankful that Darius was gone and that no one had gotten seriously hurt. Of course, Karima suffered an assault and all our lives were threatened, but in the end, no one got shot or killed. After the officer handcuffed Darius and placed him in the squad car, we all had a chance to talk. Darius had committed serious crimes and needed to be held accountable, but we also had the reputation of the program to think about. If he was arrested and processed, word would travel like an uncontrolled fire in the foothills. The whole world would find out that our life changing, history making program was marred by African Americans bringing gun violence to Africa. Not only bringing gun violence to Africa, but doing so during an attempt to rape and kidnap the visionary and founder of the program! There was simply too much at stake. We were going to have to let Darius Jones get away with felony level crimes. He agreed to a police escort to his gate and signed a non-disclosure agreement, although he obviously had nothing to gain by talking about the incident since law enforcement waived arrest and prosecution with conditions.

Having lost our appetites, Fatou and I settled into bed and hydrated ourselves with bottled water from the wet bar. We were mentally and physically exhausted although it was only about 8:30 p.m. "Well, tomorrow is day three of our trip and day two of the orientation. Even though we went through hell this evening, we know that the Lord answered our prayer to eliminate the evil force against our program and we don't have to worry about Darius anymore. As a result, we can now put our full energy into completing the orientation," Fatou offered. "Yeah, he was told that the statute of limitations is two years on his crimes and that he can be extradited if he causes more problems in the future, so I think he will leave us alone," I responded. After watching television for a while, we fell into deep, much needed sleep.

CHAPTER 46

Karima and Natu

After I filled Natu in on what happened after I got into the room, we just rested and stopped talking for a while. We were both lost in our thoughts. I was jittery and still shaken, but I felt very safe with Natu there. Gossip or no gossip, he was going to stay the night with me. I just didn't have the courage to be alone. Life hadn't been smooth sailing for me, but I had never been held at gunpoint or had a mad man threaten my life, so I was quite undone.

Nonetheless, I was not going to allow anyone to get in the way of us getting this program off the ground. By tomorrow, after a good night's sleep, I plan to hit the ground running and enjoy day two of orientation, which will consist of Senegalese history and culture. I was really looking forward to learning in-depth information about the area. Our "no name" favorite restaurant would be serving lunch to the members in addition to sharing information on popular Senegalese dishes.

Getting back to the present, even though it was for all the right reasons, I was in a situation I had planned to avoid. Namely, to avoid putting Natu and me in a position of temptation. I only had one bed in my room. After my shower, I sat on the bed where Natu lay waiting for me. Luckily, I had on legitimate old lady, two-piece pajamas. I got into bed and moved into his waiting arms.

He kissed me softly and held me in his arms. I decided to come clean rather than mislead him about my limitations in this relationship, but once I started talking and he could tell where I was going, he told me that I was free to do or not do anything I wanted to in the relationship. I liked what I heard, but I knew we needed to really spell it out and be clear with each other.

I told him about my one and only intimate experience and that I had decided that my second one would be with my husband. I admitted that I was crazy about him, but was unsure of where our relationship would go with us living on two different continents. To my surprise, he looked at me and kissed me again and said, "My love, if I can have what I want, you will be my wife. If I hadn't known that before, I knew for sure when your life was threatened today. I knew I couldn't live without you when I saw you being held at gunpoint. At that moment, I couldn't imagine my life without you and was ready to take a bullet for you. Karima, I won't pressure you or rush you, but I can tell you right now, I want you. I want to marry you and spend the rest of my life with you. I need you to think about whether you want to marry me and you let me know what you decide. I will not put any pressure on you for intimacy until you are my wife, but the sooner the better," he laughed.

I'm a blessed woman I realized. I just hugged him tighter and said, "You saved my life today. If you hadn't signaled for me to use my arm which caused him to drop the gun, I don't know what would have happened, but I believe someone would have been shot and maybe killed. As petrified as I was, a calmness came over me because you were here and also because I knew God would not allow his plan to be marred by murder and mayhem." I kissed his chest and said thank you again. "I don't have to think about it Natu, you are a Christian man and I love you. I think about you day and night. I would love to marry your newly divorced butt." We laughed hard and then went to sleep in each other's arms, exhausted by the events of the day.

CHAPTER 47

Karima

"Natu wants to take me to Dakar this weekend to buy my engagement ring Fatou!" Fatou asked, "So let me get this straight, you're getting married?" I didn't answer and just grabbed my friend and held her tight. We were in the foyer of the Warma Building where the morning session of the second day of Orientation was on break. We stepped outside.

"After all that happened to me yesterday, Natu stayed the night with me and we just talked about our relationship. I tried to set some boundaries to protect my virtue, but Natu headed me off at the pass and told me he wants to be my husband, not my boyfriend, in so many words. That was how he proposed and it worked for me." "Karima, you two look so good together. He is such a solid person. I am so happy for you. When will it happen?" I told Fatou that we were both too old for a long engagement, so the nuptials will take place before the end of the month. Fatou and I decided to have dinner together as soon as possible, just the girls, to work on the wedding plans.

By the end of "Day Two" of the Orientation, we witnessed a number of budding friendships between Nafre residents, new and old. One such interesting development was the obvious attraction between Anthony Wright of Atlanta and Fatima Chebo, the party planner. Fatou heard them make plans to drive to Dakar over the weekend so that Anthony could purchase a car. Pa Luc, a middle-aged widow and lifetime Nafre resident talked to Millicent Grays from Delaware about his life and invited her to church on Sunday. Clara Simmons and Bill Calloway went to high school together, coincidentally, and made plans for dinner this weekend. It was especially interesting how easily the people interacted so effortlessly and easily when most people would have thought cultural barriers would have thwarted such progress for months, even years.

In the afternoon session, Chief Anuna admonished the new residents that failing to greet a person in passing during the course of the day was considered an insult of the highest level. To fail to acknowledge and greet a fellow human being was considered uncivilized and highly offensive, so he implored the new people never to overlook this very basic expectation in African culture. Anthony Wright spoke up after the Chief's admonition saying, "I used to wonder why my father always spoke to other black people, whether he knew them or not, in stores, on the street, anywhere really. One day I asked him about it and he said, we were taught to acknowledge each other and to speak as part of unspoken kinship. Other peoples don't really do that except occasionally, but old school black people usually do. Now, I know where it came from." That was a real ice breaker and it prompted all kinds of interesting remarks about cross cultural similarities between Africans and African Americans, most of them funny, but still insightful.

CHAPTER 48

Karima

Since Natu was able to confirm that Darius was put on the plane by the police and that law enforcement stayed at the gate until his flight took off to make sure he didn't slink out of the airport, I felt safe in the hotel villa by myself although I moved into the empty villa next to Kofi and Fatou just in case. Natu and I had set the date of our small wedding ceremony for March thirtieth, the day after the welcome home celebration. I changed my return flight to April seventh so that we could at least spend a week together as husband and wife before I left again. On Saturday, Fatou, Fatima and I are going to Dakar to find a dress. Natu will meet me there after we're done so that we can shop for a ring. I've been trying to play it off, but I'm beside myself with excitement. Natu is a beautiful man who just oozes virility and strength. I feel overjoyed that he is mine. I've been reading healthy relationship books and articles to make sure I'm up on "best practices" for keeping a man. My lack of experience is becoming a concern for me although everything I'm reading seems to suggest there are three main components to successful relationships; showing respect, being considerate and communicating continuously. Seemed easy enough.

Natu mentioned that his ex-wife Lia called him recently. Their children had told her he was getting married. He said that she used the transfer of title on a vehicle as the reason for the call, but soon began to question him about his upcoming marriage. Specifically, she wanted to know how long he had known me, apparently trying to do the math on the length of our relationship. He told her that he met me after she sued him for divorce, but she called him a liar. I became a little bothered by it given what we had just gone through with Darius, so I asked him if we should be concerned about her. He told me that she was a spoiled brat, but relatively harmless. Still, after we had dinner together that evening and I returned to my room alone, I began to worry about it. Maybe I was moving too fast.

I had spoken to my Son and told him my good news. Hassan was very happy for me and told me that he trusted my judgment regarding marrying Natu, but he did ask me a few questions about it such as had Natu been married before? I told him about his long marriage, long separation and recent divorce. He said, "Mom, I would normally think that going from a marriage to a divorce to another marriage would be a bad idea, but from everything you told me about Natu, I believe that he genuinely loves you." He does Son, I told him. I promised Hassan that I would be returning a week late because of the wedding and that I would return to Nafre a couple of weeks after that which he accepted pretty well. We talked about everything going on with us. Apparently, my granddaughters' basketball team is likely going to the playoffs and I will be able to catch a few games while I'm home.

My thoughts drifted back to Lia, Natu's ex-wife. I hope she doesn't think I'm a homewrecker. I met the man after they had been separated for months and after she filed for divorce against him. I never even kissed him before he was divorced, but she doesn't know that. That's what worries me. I'm going to talk to Natu about this because perhaps we need to keep our plans to ourselves until we are officially married.

CHAPTER 49

Lia

How dare that bastard jump up and get married when the ink hasn't even dried on our divorce papers. This is an embarrassment to our children, our families and to the dignity of my family name. Everyone is gossiping and believes he left me for her, an American! Everyone knows they and those Europeans come over here desperate and looking for men. After everything I did for him and he throws me away like a washed up rag doll. My family put him through school and gave him a start in carpentry. Ungrateful jerk.

Because of these slave descendants moving to Senegal, everyone in our circle is asking me about Natu and looking at me with pity because he is so popular now as a leading figure in that program. I married him because I knew he was capable of greatness, but he refused to take the financial help he needed to catapult his career because it would have come from my family. He had what we call "false pride" and it costs us our family. I could no longer accept that I lived better as a child than I did as an adult because of him! We couldn't even afford house boys and I had to cook and clean up. The shame became more than I could bear and I filed for divorce, but it was all his fault. During our marriage, I lost friends and became a recluse because I didn't have the wardrobe to attend society weddings and special events. After all that, and as soon as our marriage was over, Natu became an overnight sensation, the toast of the region and appears to have a great salary. I've got to take my time and think about this.

I don't think I can live with him embarrassing me like this, twice. Also, I still love him, God help me. I miss the good parts of what we had. I am in so much pain.

I've heard about the great celebration they are planning for the Americans. I may very well buy a table for our family and introduce the community to the real Mrs. Bello.

CHAPTER 50

Darius

Not sure how things went so wrong. I had Karima all to myself and was poised to brand her as mine and, instead of her welcoming my affection, she bit me. I bared my soul to her, but she rejected me. I sit here in my near empty house, my family gone, my carefully crafted image history and all I can think about is Karima. If she had just let me love her, I believe she would have fallen for me again, but even as I formed that thought, I was also beginning to see that something was wrong with my logic.

My life as I knew it was over. I haven't even tried to see Cassidy or Arianna. I don't even know where they live and, to be honest, I don't even care at this moment. We probably all need a break from each other. I need some time to reconcile the last week of my life. I did things I didn't know I was capable of. I need to center myself and pick up the pieces.

I agreed to meet with my mother and Marilyn tomorrow. I'm happy about that, but I feel so lost now that I probably won't make a good impression. I'm very confused. I don't know why I fought with Kofi and them about the program. I know damn well that only descendants of Africa should have been able to join a Back-to-Africa program, but I tried to block them because my circle of friends might not like it and possibly think that I'm pro-Black as opposed to being color blind. I made it about me. I shouldn't have joined their Board, but I couldn't resist the opportunity to get next to Karima. One thing's for sure, I'm through with messing with that program. I am hella lucky not be in prison right now.

Had that scene played out over there the way it should have, I'd be in jail right now on another continent.

It's funny though, even here by myself in an empty house, I'm feeling a little better. My thinking is a little more clear. I can't wait to see my family, Marilyn and my Mom. I'm going to apologize for not looking for them. I plan to help them if they need it. I have spent enough years running from my past. That's over. I poured myself a drink, looked at the news and fell into a peaceful sleep.

I woke up in a great mood and tried to keep myself busy to pass the time. Five o'clock finally came. My people looked great. My Mom had aged, but she still looked attractive and energetic. Marilyn looked like a grown up version of herself. When we saw each other standing outside the landmark steak house restaurant I told them to meet me at, there was no issue of recognition, we just ran towards each other and cried, all of us, while holding each other. When we got it back together, we went inside and took our booth. I sat on one side and they sat together on the other side. That was perfect for me because I was able to just look at them. I surprised myself because I became that little boy again. We just kind of picked up where we left off, but at the point before Mom fell to drugs.

A funny thing happened, I told them the truth. That's not to say that I told them everything because I certainly left out Karima, Africa and the Motherland Bound program, but I did tell them about Cassidy and Arianna. I even told them that they left me and that I had been cruel to my wife. That's when they dropped a bombshell on me and told me that they had been in touch with Cassidy for nearly a year after she found them! I wanted to get upset about it and lambaste Cassidy to them, but I couldn't because I was so glad to have my family back. After more conversation, I could see that Cassidy was not my enemy. In fact, she had been a friend to a husband who never honored her from day one. Sure, I had taken care of her, but I showed her no respect. I also told them that I had been far less than a good father, painting a false and inauthentic picture of myself to my daughter. I asked Marilyn and my Mom to help me repair my life. I could tell they loved me unconditionally and would do anything for me. I wasn't going to try and reconcile with Cassidy though because I love a different woman. Even though Karima is not mine at this point, I still want her, so I won't insult Cassidy further by trying to lure her back into a loveless marriage just to restore familiarity to my life. Those few moments of holding Karima in my arms were so special to me. I will never get over her.

My mother asked me to forgive her for ruining our childhoods. With a lot of pain and emotion, she told us that she had fallen in love with a neighborhood man who she never brought around us. That man, as it turns out, did not really love her and convinced her to experiment with the drugs he used regularly. She said she had resisted for several weeks, but she had fallen in love with him and finally broke down and tried crack in order to please and keep him. Soon after that, she got hooked and everything fell apart, paving the way for child neglect charges. She told me that she went into rehabilitation as part of her court-mandated plan to get us back, but she backslid and failed. Although it hurt to hear the story, it did something for me. After my conduct in Africa, I understood the power of love. The pure human truth of her story had touched me and I forgave her because I knew she had been a great, involved mother before that happened. Even before she told me what happened, I had already torn down the walls of anger and resentment against my mother. I let her know that I forgave her.

An even bigger fear for me had been what happened to Marilyn. I was very worried that she had winded up in an abusive foster home while I enjoyed the perks of the Smith household. I braced myself for her story. To my great surprise, I learned that Marilyn had been placed in a Christian home just as I had been, and the real kind, not lip service Christianity. Marilyn has a foster sister with whom she is still close. She graduated with honors from high school and even attended college for a couple of years.

Marilyn used her resources and found our mother at a time when she had been clean and sober for three years. They decided to move to Las Vegas together where the cost of living was low and where there were no state taxes. My mom even found a good job as a peer counselor at a drug rehabilitation program. I was very proud of both of them. They followed me home but didn't stay the night because there were really no beds to sleep in. They had a hotel room, so it really didn't matter. At that point, I had them back in my life and planned to see them as often as possible. I was no longer worried about what to tell Cassidy and Arianna. I would just tell them the truth.

Before I went to sleep that night, I did something I hadn't done in a long time, I got on my knees and prayed. I thanked the Lord for saving me from myself in Africa. I asked for forgiveness for what I tried to do to Karima and I told the Lord that I would treat her with respect once I was able to get her back. I pledged to support my mother and sister in every possible way. I also asked the Lord to heal my mind from guilt for not finding my family and for erasing their memory with lies. Finally, I promised the Lord that I would be fair with Cassidy in the divorce and that I would become the father that my daughter deserved, in Jesus' name.

CHAPTER 51

King and Queen

"Charles, I cannot wait until the end of this day since it is the last day of orientation. For one thing, I want that deed, but I think I want the information to get my business started just as much," Bridgette said. "On my laptop, I have already designed the floor plan and decor. I also developed my menu which will include sandwiches and other healthy dishes besides pressed juice and smoothies. I just hope I can get a ground level unit." "I wonder what rent will look like?" Charles asked, not really expecting an answer. He continued, "In the States, they call setting the space up for the business, "a build out." I'm pretty sure we have to pay for that." "Yeah, I've been worried about that too, but I'm hoping that we won't be under tight regulations over here because that's what forces up the costs of a build out. Anyway, let's stop worrying and hope for the best," said Bridgette.

Sitting on their comfortable sofa enjoying a cup of coffee, Charles thought about the earlier conversation with Bridgette. I will use all my construction skills to set up my wife's business, but I plan to get on with the solar outfit instead of starting a business of my own, I confirmed with myself. I've always been interested in living "off the grid" and in conserving the earth's resources. Hopefully, I can provide the company additional support with my sales skills since they can sell solar energy commercially or to residential customers. Look at me, sitting here about to start guaranteed and desirable employment, but also supporting my wife in starting the business of her dreams just a few days out from leaving a homeless encampment. I got up to "test" the latest dessert recipe prepared by Bridgette in order to narrow down the choices for her menu. This one was a lemon curd bar with a graham cracker crust. I was going to gain weight if she kept this going because I couldn't resist her exceptional culinary creations. There was little doubt her business would be successful. Her baking talent was one of the many things I didn't know about Bridgette before due to our unorthodox living situation in the States.

Later that afternoon, we returned home and immediately started going through all the paperwork for registering the business and for choosing a location after we put our deed in a safe place. Before we started on the papers, we literally stopped and looked at each other. We put the papers down and held each other. "God is with us baby. I'm so fortunate to have you girl...." We laughed because my words mid-sentence turned into a song as I did my best "Maxwell" impression. Bridgette swooned with me and we just slow danced with no music. My cell phone rang and it was Shay, my son's mother. "Great timing," I said to myself sarcastically before answering the phone.

"Charles, you're going to have to come and get Jr. I've met somebody I plan to marry who's in the military and I'm moving to the base in Iraq. I don't want to take Jr. because my fiancé thinks it would be better for Jr. to be with you," she said. Completely shocked but overjoyed to hear what she said, I recovered fast saying, "No problem Shay, I can get back out there within a week to get him. Is that okay?" "I guess it will have to be although I need to leave here on April fifth," she replied. "I know he has a passport and I'll arrange for his VISA. I'll get there as soon as I get a ticket which I'll start working on right now and I'll text my arrival date and time to you. Please tell Little Man I'll be there soon and thank you Shay for trusting me with him. You know I'll take care of him and you'll see him whenever you can." "I appreciate that Charles. You were always a great father. I can't deny that. I just need a chance to find happiness like you did and I know our son will be happy if he's with you. He cries for you and asks for you all the time," she admitted.

After we hung up, I told Bridgette what she said and Bridgette was ecstatic. Right away, we got on the Internet and found reasonably priced tickets out of Dakar on Monday morning. With the savings we both had, we bought my round trip ticket and Jr.'s one-way ticket. We should be back here by Wednesday, God willing. Come to think about it, I needed to get back a.s.a.p. and get on that solar plant payroll since our money was running low all of a sudden. It was going to help a lot that I had already completed the application process and had a start date of April seventh.

That evening in bed, although I was so relieved to know my son would be with me after all, the guilt I had been carrying for leaving him was sitting on my chest like a ton of bricks. I cursed myself for being so bad off that I had to leave the country and my son to get an opportunity. Once again however, God had come through clutch, like some kind of corporate fixer, and cleaned up my mess. I vowed to never leave my child again under any circumstances. I wanted to judge Shay for her choices, but I wasn't any better than her really except for the dire circumstances I was in. I asked God to forgive me for my weaknesses and thanked him for returning my flesh and blood to me.

By that Wednesday evening, my son and I arrived in Nafre. Bridgette had decorated Jr.'s room and cooked us a fish fry complete with fries, fritters and cole slaw. I literally cried, I was so happy to have my boy with me. Bridgette was very loving and accepting of him even though it was the first time she had ever seen him. We "FaceTimed" Shay so she could see Jr. and talk to him. Little Man gave her a tour of our home and his new room on the camera feature of his phone. It was all good. That night, I got the best sleep of my entire life. I was home and I had my family with me. I had a deed to my home and my home was in Africa, the land of my soul.

CHAPTER 52

Natu

All I have to do is make it to March thirtieth. Karima has no idea what being around her is doing to me. I mean I know she can tell I want her, but she has no idea how much. March thirtieth can't come soon enough. Once our lives are joined, I'm not sure how I'm supposed to live my life with my wife away most of the time. I'll wait until after our wedding before I broach the subject of where we are going to live after the wedding. I know she has her family in the States as well as her home, but I can't see myself leaving my country to live in America. Many Africans would jump at the chance to move to America, but I'm not one of them. America can't compete with the love I have for our land, our history or our culture. Men are taught to protect their land, their women and children. My father instilled those responsibilities in me from small. Along with most of my brothers and sisters, the ingrained appreciation we have for our land completes us. It makes us who we are. Those of us bonded to the land can't live apart from its unique terrain and the beauty of our part of the earth nor from our balanced lifestyles or the great dishes that feed and grow our nation. For my Karima though, I would spend a few months of the year with her in Arizona and that is what I
intend to propose to her.

Lia is on the warpath because I plan to remarry so soon after our divorce. I'm not particularly proud of it either, but I will not lose this opportunity to spend the rest of my life with someone I am so naturally bonded to. It's more than just attraction, although that helps a lot, it's because we are of the same mind. We both want our lives to have meaning and we don't mind working to make it happen. We support each other, not tear each other down. We also have magnetic chemistry between us. We can't keep our hands off each other. We have a lot to look forward to.

I'm going to drive to Dakar and talk to my children about my plans on Wednesday because I don't want them to misunderstand what's going on. They're adults, but if their mother is in pain, they will be too. I owe them an explanation.

CHAPTER 53

Patrice, Clara and Aliyah

"I was barely able to pull Aliyah from that water play area today", said Clara as she and Aliyah came through the kitchen door of our new home. "She's made a few new friends and wanted to play in the water and swing all day," Clara said. "Mom, thanks for dealing with her while I put down the floor in my salon. It's only 150 x 300, but I'm going to make it work," I said.

After dinner, I laid down on my bed. I never thought my cosmetology certification was going to be useful again because of how I spent the last five years, but it was. I always loved using my skills to beautify and make women feel good about themselves. I was glad I had the presence of mind to bring all my equipment like my blow dryers, flat irons and curlers. I not only did all the usual chemical work, including perms and color, but I also braided hair and cultivated natural hair styles which were fairly new in West Africa. I'm going to start with two stations and a wash area. Hopefully, I can find a stylist from the area to join me in the business. Shampoos and conditioners will be purchased locally as a boon to the local economy. I think I'll do well since local women won't have to travel to Dakar or Banjul to get their hair done. Shoot, if we mess around and get a good reputation, women from the wider area may seek us out. I opted for the smaller space to save money, but I'll get a larger one if we get popular.

Anthony helped me nail down the floors. Tomorrow, the plumbing fixtures will be installed. I'm going to create an accent wall starting with a light shade of yellow, which will grow progressively darker by the time it reaches the baseboards. I want it to be bright and fresh. Paint is fairly cheap, but it can have major design impact and that's what I'm looking for.

There is a local man by the name of Bola Cupps who introduced himself to me and offered to show me around the area. I politely declined under the guise of getting the salon ready. He seemed nice enough and I could use a friend, but it's just too soon for me to be talking to men. I was forming a little crush on Anthony after we met him at Kennedy Airport, but I believe he is sweet on Fatima. Better for me that way I figured so I can stay focused on my salvation.

I was formally baptized on Sunday and I declared to myself that I am a new woman in the Lord. "He's the only free psychiatrist known throughout the world, for solving all the problems of men, women, little boys and girls," according to Stevie Wonder's, "Have a Talk with God." I believe that. Moving forward with my life and accepting the forgiveness bestowed by grace is my game plan. I won't look back. If I find love and want to marry, I will tell that person about my past, but if I get any hint of judgment, I'll dust myself off and move on because God forgives me, I don't need another person to validate me.

I joined my mother in the backyard as she watered her plants. "Patrice, those rosemary and lettuce seeds Aliyah and I planted are already starting to sprout. Would you believe that I am starting to feel better since starting the plant based diet over here," Clara said. "Sure I believe it. Even though we still eat fish, we are getting very fresh, straight out of the ocean seafood, so I don't feel guilty about that at all. What I noticed after I stopped eating meat was that the pain from fibroids went away and I believe they shrank. I did a little research and confirmed that it was a possibility. Apparently, eating the wrong foods can literally kill you and cause all kinds of adverse reactions in the body," I said. "A lot of what we have eaten historically started in times of slavery. Even though we made delicacies out of the worst parts of animals and the scraps we were given, those foods became the foundation of our diets for centuries leaving us to suffer early onset of chronic, preventable conditions," Mom said. "I hope it's not too late for me to reverse the effects of my bad choices." "It's not," I assured her.

After that, we sat in silence, breathing in the fresh air. The homes were built in circles and there were no fences. Since our three-bedroom home was in the innermost and first circle of homes, there was a large section in the middle where the park and common areas were located. Mom had received permission to use a half-acre of that land to establish a community garden.

"I ordered a tiller on "Amazon" to start breaking down the land for the garden, but was able to cancel it because Bill Calloway loaned me one. I still cannot get over the coincidence of both of us from Mt. Mary High School winding up out here connected to the same program," Clara said. "Moms, I believe the man is sweet on you. Do you like, like him," I asked? "Bill is good people and I do like him, but I'm not ready for like, like, as you say. Right now, I've just got to get used to being here and I've got to do me; get my weight down, my blood pressure down and so forth. I brought my scale and my blood pressure monitor and the numbers are already going in the right direction, so I'm not going to tempt fate out here worrying about a man, at least not yet. In the meantime, Bill is a trustworthy family friend and he is welcome to be around us when he has time, but we'll just focus on our friendship for now."

After my bath, nightly meditation and prayers, I slathered peppermint oil all over my body. The clean but strong scent kept my nostrils clear and my mind focused. We had been here just over a week and Africa had not disappointed at all. My first hair appointment would be next week. I couldn't wait to get going. Mom, Aliyah and I needed to start thinking about what we're going to wear to the welcome home celebration. The whole idea of it was mind-boggling. I never fathomed such a thing. No standing US president had even apologized to us for what was done to us, let alone compensated for slavery or for centuries of crippling discrimination and racism. We never got that "forty acres and a mule." And yes, while many of us are "balling," the majority of us still live near the poverty line in America. Our dignity is assaulted daily and we just have to absorb it and suck it up at the expense of our emotional health. That is no way to live. So, all of that gives the welcome home celebration very special meaning because, finally, someone is acknowledging our perilous plight and saying, "We see you, we want you, welcome home." Yeah, it means a lot.

If Aliyah grows to love this land, marries and has children here, they will become native Africans and our family genealogy will return to its roots. What a divine blessing that would be!

CHAPTER 54

Anthony

Fatima kind of pulled a fast one on me. She agreed to go to Dakar with me to find a car, but she didn't tell me that she had to meet with Karima and Fatou, the Founders, to look for a wedding dress for Karima. I winded up at some bridal salon with them for over an hour. It really wasn't that bad though. Karima fell in love with the fourth dress she tried on and it was beautiful on her I had to admit. Women love those kinds of things, we men would rather be doing anything but something like that, but I'm still glad I did it. You learn a lot about women that way.

For instance, I observed how stylish and genuine Fatima is. I love women with swag and a lot of confidence. Before I left the States, I was noticing how a lot of women without any health related reasons are doing the most with all the fake hair, nails and lashes. Even implants are common. If they take all that stuff off, you don't even recognize them. Some are far more beautiful without all that extra stuff, I just wish they knew it. Men can take a lot of responsibility for putting pressure on women to try and achieve a certain kind of look in order to be attractive to them. We all need to pay attention to our appearances and presentation, but true beauty comes from within and enhances the external. A confident and warm woman with her own personal style, not given to gimmicks and fads, is the bomb in my book. That's how Fatima rolls and I'm feeling her. Sitting there in that bridal salon, I actually thought about how beautiful she would look in one of those dresses. I knew I had to get out of there then. Thank goodness, Karima finished up and Fatima and I left together and found a place to eat.

We looked around at about four lots in the middle of the city and I purchased a five speed, 2010 Toyota. Fatima said that about half the cars on the road in Senegal have manual transmissions. I was glad that Pops had taught me to drive them because the automatics cost more. Once I got the car, we headed back to Nafre in separate cars. We couldn't stay together after that because Fatima had to get back to work on the welcome celebration. On the ride to Dakar, she told me a lot about her background. She grew up in Nafre and moved to New York to attend school and also did some modeling while she was there, which explains her sophisticated look. After a few years in New York though, she grew tired of the fast pace and wanted to return home to try and bring Nafre into the new world. She said she could not believe her luck when the Motherland Bound program chose Nafre as their pilot location. It was just the break she needed, she said.

I wanted to crack for a chance to be her man right then, but I was scared to just jump right into that kind of conversation without first gauging her feelings for me. I managed to say, "Fatima, I would love to spend time with you and have you show me the wider area. No pressure though." She didn't respond right away, so I was feeling really stupid for opening my mouth, but then she said, "Anthony, I would love to show you around and hang out together. When the celebration is over, I am going to have you over and cook a lovely meal for you if you would like." "I can't wait," I said with a goofy grin on my face.

CHAPTER 55

Karima

I decided to venture out to the beach alone and reflect since I had the whole day to myself. Natu went to Dakar to see his children today. Fatou and Kofi flew home to Ghana for a few days. I packed a nice lunch for myself of "California Rolls" from the hotel restaurant, mineral water, nuts and fresh fruit. The hotel's private beach was breathtaking. There was a nearby bar, comfortable lounge chairs, a souvenir shop, white sand and other amenities. The music in the background included reggae, Afro-beat, easy listening and R&B. It was loud enough to hear, but not loud enough to interfere with your thoughts or conversations.

Quiet as it's kept, that episode with Darius still has me spooked. I've just got to make it to my wedding night when my husband will have a permanent spot in any bed I'm in. Until then, I've been having Natu check my room each night before I go in and I place the dresser in front of the door for extra security once he leaves. In my right mind, I know that Darius has "left the building," but I'm still a little frightened that he might return. He had full on rape on his mind that day. Did he think that was going to *make* me love him? I thank the Holy Spirit for urging me to be still which is what gave me a chance to jump off of him and scream. Apparently, the men were right outside the door at the same moment I screamed and they were able to get inside and subdue him, eventually. Maybe two minutes, if that, passed between the men barging in and them taking Darius down, but it seemed like two hours. If they hadn't been there, he would have succeeded. And what was he going to do with me afterwards? It's too scary to think about. What would have happened if Natu had barged in and caught him in the act? He might have killed him since he had his own gun. Would he have thought less of me for being soiled by another man right before we were to marry? My spirit is bruised by what Darius did. I don't even want to think about what would have happened to my spirit if he had succeeded. I really doubt I would be here at the beach relaxing and thinking about my impending wedding and the welcome home celebration. I just sat quietly and coaxed my mind to think of more pleasant things.

Our wedding day is just four days away. My wedding dress is gorgeous. They say your wedding dress should make you feel like a princess and the one I chose certainly had me feeling like royalty. I had waited until after I received my "AARP" card to get married, so I didn't feel guilty about getting the dress of my dreams which is an elegant, simple, sleeveless, pencil style dress in pure white silk with pearl piping along the neckline, bodice, arms and hem, which gleamed against my brown skin. The thing that plagued me was not having my family with me at my wedding. Hassan told me over the phone last night that the girls are really bummed about it although still really happy for me. Once Natu gets his green card and travels to Phoenix, we will have a special reception for the family. That's about all I can do to rectify the situation.

This weekend will be one of the busiest and most monumental of my life. The welcome home celebration for the business I founded is Saturday and our wedding is on the next day. That's less than one week away. Fatou promised to be my matron of honor and Fatima will "beat" and help me get prepared. I plan to ask Patrice to style my hair at her new salon. We have ten new businesses starting in Nafre within a week as a result of our push on the last day of orientation. I believe several more new businesses are in the works. Clara told me about the community garden she established where all the Nafre homeowners, new and old, will work together on choosing plants and dividing maintenance duties. Patrice also arranged showings of "Nollywood" movies in the Warma Bldg. twice a month for a small donation which will benefit the community garden! It just makes me giggle witnessing our collective dreams evolve in sync.

Sometimes I feel like I'm dreaming when I think about all these things. I mean, far less than a year ago, I was huffing and puffing around with that extra weight on me, getting played at the job and going nowhere fast in my life. How do you process all this change in so little time? I remembered that "God has given every believer "a measure of faith." "Measure your value by how much faith God has given you." Romans 12:3. I would like to believe that he gave me a nice dose of faith in him to step out as I did, but I could never undervalue the role and contribution of Fatou and Kofi and start thinking I did it all by myself. If they hadn't been looking for a way to serve others, none of this would have happened. I've got to make sure that Fatima showers them with accolades and praise at the event for the faith they demonstrated. I am forever in their debt.

Speaking of the celebration, Fatou and I plan to come correct for the party. When I was in Dakar, I picked up two dresses; one for the celebration and the other, my wedding dress. Fatou is going to have something very special made for herself in Accra for the event. With the celebration taking place the night before my wedding, I've got to do everything in my power to get a good night sleep on Saturday night to be ready for Sunday. I don't want bags under my eyes down to my knees on my wedding day. I want to look as young and fresh as I can when I marry the love of my life.

I thought about my Sweetie. I know he's seeing his children today. I think he is going to tell them about me. I hate to think I have caused them any pain. None of us lives in a vacuum though. The things we do affect our families and our loved ones and we have to remain mindful of that. They have the right to know what is going on and why their father is marrying again so soon. I believe it will all work out because Natu and I took every precaution to do things as God would have them.

I got a call from a number in Dakar and I picked up. No one spoke on the other end though. I have no idea who it could have been since my name is becoming well known because of the program. I truly hope it was not Natu's wife which was my best guess unfortunately. The only people who know about the wedding are Natu's children, Fatou, Kofi, Fatima, Anthony and the Elders and I'm going to keep it that way. I have fallen deeply in love with my future husband and nothing will stop us from marrying.

As the morning turned to afternoon, I was very relaxed and mesmerized by the rhythm of the splashing waves against the shore. Taking advantage of this free time to meditate and plan prospectively, I wondered to myself how many people we would ultimately re-settle here by the time it was all said and done. It may be that there is a finite number of people we can accommodate financially. I just pray that supply and demand will match up, at least roughly. Undoubtedly, most African Americas are not going to want to leave the States and come here, but how much longer will they consider a place home where they feel rejected by the majority and have the cloud of racism hanging over their heads at all times? Since I got here, another unarmed black man was killed by police in America for a routine traffic stop. Protest and unrest followed. In other words, the same repetitive, knee jerk pattern. Killing, protest, no change; killing, protest, no change.

Even still, leaving the only place you know for a different continent, thousands of miles away, is no small thing. In fact, because of my fastly approaching wedding to an African man, I'm going to be forced to make a decision myself about where to live. Right about now, I'm feeling pretty good over here. The vibe is easy going, welcoming and uncannily familiar. It's amazing how the sensibilities of the Africans and the African Americans are so similar. That cannot be a coincidence. We just fell right in with each other. Our basic countenance as a people, that even keeled, magnanimous spirit we have is genetic at this point, formed from the beginning of humankind on this earth. When you think about the thousands of years it takes to form a culture, it's not surprising that the same peoples would have similar ways even after being separated for four hundred or so years. We love showing respect to each other. We'll call an older person Miss, Mr., Auntie, even after we become adults consistent with "home training." In fact, in some parts of Africa, the mother is called by the name of her children such as "Hassan Ma." Humor is our default mode of communication as a people and we take God very seriously, by and large. Of course, challenges have affected our fundamental nature and some of us have reacted badly to adversity and fallen off course trying to survive untenable circumstances, but that does not change our foundational mindset. Bottom line, I fit in here. I don't feel out of place. I feel complete.

But how can I leave my son, my only child in America and move here? How could I not see my girls grow up and not have regular influence on them or miss their exciting basketball games? This is going to be tough. I hope Natu will be willing to spend parts of the year in both places. Even if he is though, what about his job over here? We're still in the early stages of building and he is the project manager. It may be that I will be traveling back and forth most of the time. I'll have to be good with that for the first year or two if that is what is required. Natu and I aren't kids anymore. We'll make the necessary sacrifices to keep our marriage healthy without either of us being entirely torn from our families.

CHAPTER 56

Then the LORD said to him, "Know for certain that for four hundred years your descendants will be strangers in a country not their own and that they will be enslaved and mistreated there. But I will punish the nation they serve as slaves, and afterward they will come out with great possessions. You, however, will go to your ancestors in peace and be buried at a good old age. In the fourth generation your descendants will come back here, for the sin of the Amorites has not yet reached is full measure."
- Genesis 15:13-16 NIV

Fatima

March 29, 2019, City of Nafre, Country of Senegal, Continent of Africa

The cars we hired just left Dakar with a gang of American and West African celebrities I told Anthony. He has been helping me with all the last minute tasks to be ready for tonight. Our programs arrived and they are spectacular. True keepsakes. I have a feeling people may be interested in collecting them, so we may be able to raise more money for the programs if we sell them after the fact. All the robes have arrived and they were inspected for quality control. No shortcomings whatsoever were found. That's that African perfectionism! The tables were set and will be the talk of the town. Can you imagine the picture of all fifty African American new residents in their glorious, majestic robes. One for posterity indeed. Right now, the musicians and the singers are rehearsing and the sound system is on point.

Classic Senegalese dishes will be served to all guests of honor, dignitaries, celebrities and staff. There will be food vendors for local Africans who come to pay homage to their returning brethren. Elder Whey will handle the "run of show" to ensure that speakers and acts observe their time limits. Africans are notorious for ignoring clocks and go with the flow instead. African Americans call it "CP" time, or colored people's time. However, tonight, they are going to have to keep it moving because pay scales require we end on time or blow our budget. Plus, you always want to keep people wanting more.

I returned to my home to change into a gown specially made for this event by a local designer. She used purple taffeta with gold piping for the dress and created a headdress similar to the one Queen Nefertiti wore in ancient times. Anthony picked me up and took me back to the site of the event. I'm so glad my man has a car. Yes, my man. After our day trip to Dakar a couple of weeks ago, he cooked dinner for me returning the favor of the special meal I prepared for him before that. After we enjoyed the meal he prepared, we were just talking in his kitchen. Then, he just stared at me pensively, but his gaze morphed into a look of pure desire and suddenly we just ran into each other's arms and kissed like I had never been kissed before. We have become very close and I am absolutely crazy about him. My father had a lot of questions about him, but I assured Dad that Anthony was smart, ambitious and committed to our relationship. Anthony told me about his desire to pay ball again and I am going to do everything I can to support his dream.

Finally, everything was in place. Elder Whey was quite the taskmaster and had everyone lined up where they were supposed to be to run the show. You've got to remember, this is the person who oversaw the entire group family move and the welcome center kick off event. The woman is able. She met with the same result at this welcome home celebration, flawless execution.

A. YVONNE STOKES

Afrobeat classics started the show, instruments only. We couldn't even get to the welcome greeting and first speaker before people were partying and dancing in the aisles. It was becoming obvious that people were in their feelings. As a people, we have never really addressed our pain and others have not acknowledged it. It was starting to look like tonight's event would give many of us an opportunity to express our feelings, in person or via television. There were cameras everywhere from all the major African, American, South American, European and Caribbean networks. The atmosphere was electric. The crowd was united.

The African American Motherland Bound members appeared to be enjoying themselves, including Anthony, but were kind of stoic at the same time. I guess they felt self-conscious being the center of attention for joining a relocation program, which happened to be connected to one of the most astounding tragedies in human history. I'm proud that they were all willing to come and participate.

Elder Whey had the band to segue to softer music and Karima was introduced. She delivered a riveting speech, which summarized our history from ancient times to the present. She implored Africans from all over the world to be proud of their heritage and to resist internalizing rejection by ignorant, hateful people who would self-exalt themselves over Africans and other people who don't look like them. Finally, she challenged all of us to prepare the continent for the betterment of future generations by overcoming the sin of selfishness and by being courageous. Karima was a hard act to follow, but the other speakers were also remarkable and prolific with their words and in delivery. The entertainers were at their best in every way, including their costumes, song selection and performance. We even had two comedians in between acts whose ethnic comedy tore the house down. The show ran for a total of two and a half hours.

We had a "pop up" feature on the screen for comments by viewers from around the world, and boy, some of them were profound. One viewer from Brazil, translated, wrote, "I never thought I'd live to see the day when black people had the audacity to proclaim their place in the world and unapologetically say, we will validate ourselves." An African American wrote in, "I only wish my parents had lived to see this show. What I saw and heard today changed my life. I am so proud of our ancestors for surviving and making a way for us. I could never be ashamed of them for being slaves. The slave owners should own the shame."

During the meal, we enjoyed the sounds of neo-soul and a slide show, which chronicled the inception of the Motherland Bound program to present day. It was funny at times because Karima even allowed us to show a "before" picture of her before her weight loss and the new image she carved out after she left her employer due to being fired. The girl looked good even "before." The "pop up" subtitles had an explanation or story for every picture and the crowd not only got a kick out of it, but they also learned the history of the program.

At the end of the show, there was a prayer for tolerance and world peace. Everyone took lighters strategically placed at the top of their place settings and lit a flame in honor of our long-suffering and strong ancestors. When the show was over, the only problem we had was trying to get people to leave the grounds. They just couldn't get enough of the family atmosphere and the ambiance. The television ratings and the ratings of other mediums were not confirmed, but easily more than twenty million people had viewed the broadcast all over the world. It kind of felt like the world as we knew it was changing.

The breakdown and clean-up crew kicked in. Many attendees and guests stayed around to help, including Anthony and I. When we got home, we just laid out on my sectional and relaxed. It was done. I was relieved that it went so well. All there was left to do now was live our lives.

CHAPTER 57

Spirit

The splendor and pageantry of the welcome home celebration took me back to my days on earth in Ancient Egypt. The spoken word artist, Keya, delivered her words to the sounds of "Nights Over Egypt," by the Jones Girls, and the music really captured the pulse of those times. God's spirit had elevated each performer's gift to the point of faultlessness. Not only achieving technical perfection, the performances took the audience to a state of bliss, with each listener receiving each performer's gift in their souls.

I observed the delirious reactions and overtures of all in attendance, but I especially watched the fifty Africans from America who laid aside all fear and doubt in their decision to return to the homeland of their ancestors. Not really knowing what to expect, they took their seats on the lower stage as they looked out at the hundreds of people there to cradle them in their collective bosoms of love and unconditional acceptance. Over the evening, the audience came to represent Mother Africa and the African Americans, the returning abducted children.

I had seen not only the brutality of slavery and the appurtenant death, but the unconscionable separation of parents and children as well. Africans were snatched from the very essence of their being consisting of God, country and family, only to land in the Americas, lost and confused. Then, to ultimately deduce that you were not even fully accepted as human by a people who looked to you like aliens from another planet, had to be demoralizing in every sense. So, I was watching the new residents for signs that they really understood what they had gained by returning home. They did not disappoint me. Bridgette King listened attentively to every speaker and got everyone on their feet during the rich musical performances until a student from Ghana recited a poem called, "Waiting for You," dedicated to the fifty newly restored Africans which read:

"Waiting for You"

We Have Been Waiting for You Sons and Daughters,
Your Plight Has Never Been Forgotten or Ignored,
It Goes Without Saying that Your Life Matters,
And You Deserve So Much More,
We Had Our Hands Full Over Here at Home,
Trying to Keep Our Land and Defeat Colonialism and Apartheid,
But They Only Served to Strengthen Our Countenance,
And Someway, We Found the Strength to Survive,
    You Bloomed Where You were Planted,
    And Marveled the World as You Began to Thrive,
    Welcome Home Sons and Daughters,
    Your Return Has Made Us Whole,
    Let Us Redeem Mother Africa,
    With Righteous Spiritual Strength That is Bold.

Bridgette hung on every word of the student as she recited her inspirational poem until the speaker spoke of the strength to survive, at which point Bridgette fell apart and sobbed the tears of a million years. She was not alone. Her tears brought the house down. It seemed like everyone was crying. The music changed, becoming softer and soothing for a few minutes. A local minister came up and delivered a prayer of salvation for Blacks and all people all over the world, all races, all religions. He encouraged everyone to take heart as the "Lord will never leave or forsake us." Deuteronomy 31:6. After that, people gathered themselves as the tempo of the music increased.

Then, Charles King grabbed Bridgette and stepped up to the main stage and they "danced like David!" Everyone in attendance joined them and danced to the rhythms of the Afro Beat led by popular artist, Zelo. They danced on both stages, in the aisles and even on tops of tables. The music kept them dancing for over twenty minutes while pictures of African peoples, from different eras, appeared on the screens with "pop up" summaries of the names and events to the immense pleasure of the audience. It was a stunning reminder of what we had been able to accomplish during the centuries of abject calamity. If we didn't celebrate ourselves in this way, then who would?

Tribal dancers took to the stage and re-ignited the crowd. Little Aliyah and Little Man jumped out of their chairs and joined the dancers on the main stage. To everyone's surprise, they were able to keep up with some of the dance moves. The clips of the children went viral all over the world and became the face of the celebration. Patrice and Clara retrieved the children after a few minutes and allowed them to continue dancing near their tables within arm's reach.

Yele, a Gambian comedian kept the crowd upbeat and entertained between acts. He made a few jokes at the expense of the African Americans like when he called Anthony "the center for the Nafre Nuckleheads." The evening was anointed by God. While no party or celebration could erase our deep wounds or make us whole again, it did serve a purpose. It acknowledged a tragedy and honored a remarkable occurrence, the formal return of our brethren to the land. The celebration was an icebreaker. It started a conversation about what happened to us. I was thankful to attend and anxious to witness the continued unfolding of the Motherland Bound program.

CHAPTER 58

Natu

We just witnessed history in real time. The most compelling part of the show for me was the draping of the robes and presentation of the scrolls to the new residents. When Karima read from the text printed on each Motherland Bound Inaugural Membership Certificate, a hush moved over the guests and a silent, psychic prayer ascended to the Creator.

They all cried and so did most of the audience. There were media representatives and reporters everywhere. The event will be telecast all over the world and will be talked about for years to come. The ample flood lights in all the different colors set a tone for drama and tranquility at the same time. The speakers, dancers and musical entertainment were all next level. The presentations were anointed I could say. It just seemed like everyone spoke or performed at their absolute best. It's just hard to believe what Africans have been through for the past several centuries. Nobody but God can right the wrongs but, tonight, it seems like some degree of reconciliation had been achieved. I was very proud of all of us for celebrating a victory which is what our program represents. Karima looked like a queen. She had on a designer full length gown that was iridescent, forest green. It was a kind of a form fitting wrap and it showed off her gorgeous figure. The color was perfect for her and she had a glow about her. I could hardly take my eyes off her. I was so proud of her.

Sadly, Lia showed up and tried to conjure up drama at the celebration. She was dressed like a movie star and was pretending we were still together. She had purchased an entire table and brought our children, her parents, her sister and brother. Our circle of friends is rather large so we both knew a lot of the people in attendance. Naturally, being a manager with the program, I worked the event and sat with Karima every free moment I had. To my chagrin, however, Lia had saved a seat for me next to her and practically begged me to sit there although I wouldn't. Finally, in private, my daughter told her to knock it off and she appeared to comply.

That wasn't it though. After Lia drank too much wine, she got in my face and told me that she was going to expose Karima as an adulteress and started looking for her. There was no way I was going to let her basically turn out the welcome home celebration with nonsense. Our adult children overheard her, saw where she was headed and turned her right around mid-step as she tried to approach the head table. I was really glad I talked to them beforehand and let them know that Karima did not break up their parents. After our meeting on Wednesday, they told me that they had looked up the divorce papers and now knew for sure that Lia had started the case before Karima even arrived in Senegal last fall. Lia had told them the complete opposite. They thanked me for caring about their feelings and for explaining everything to them. They would not attend the wedding to keep the peace with Lia and also to make sure that she did not show up to create drama for me. I told them I understood.

Unfortunately, Karima had seen her approaching the table and instinctively knew what was going on. She didn't know what Lia looked like, but she saw me looking distressed, appearing to chase an attractive woman with three other people following me. Fortunately, Karima stayed put seeing that we were able to re-route her in the other direction. I'm quite sure Karima will have a lot of questions for me about what happened, but this is the night before our wedding, so I won't be able to talk to her tonight. I pray that we don't spend our wedding night talking about my ex-wife.

CHAPTER 59

Karima

Natu and I jumped the broom on the beach at Victoria's! Our reception will be a small dinner at Victoria's best restaurant with Fatou, Kofi, Fatima, Anthony and all the Elders. We will spend our honeymoon in Dakar for two nights at Montell's Hotel known for its ultra-modern decor and fine dining. My bag is packed with lovely lingerie, snack foods and my best casual outfits.

The wedding was officiated by a local pastor. Our guests sat in chairs facing the ocean as Natu and I faced each other in front of them, just feet from the splashing waves. An ornate, beautiful rug below our feet kept the sand and water at bay for those few moments. Fatou and Fatima had managed to decorate the chairs with lovely tropical, exotic flowers. Natu and I recited our vows to each other and declared our love for each other. It was so special. I will never forget our oh so lovely wedding.

After the ceremony, I went to my room and changed into my after ceremony outfit of a winter white skinny legged pantsuit with pearl and gold accessories and ivory shoes. The others made their way over to the restaurant. Natu came with me to the room. Since we were officially married, I changed my clothes in front of him, which apparently hadn't been the best idea. When I got down to my risqué undergarments, he lost it and tried to jump my bones. I said, "Easy boy, there will be time later" and, though disappointed, he got it together. I had to chuckle to myself. I couldn't blame the man for trying and I was very pleased that he wanted me that badly. I certainly was looking forward to our honeymoon as well, but I wasn't going to show up at the reception table looking suspect in front of our dignified guests.

Natu and I joined our reception at the restaurant twenty minutes later. We were seated at a large table adjacent to a glass wall with an ocean view. The Chief had ordered a couple of bottles of sparking wine. The setting was absolutely breathtaking. I proudly wore my ring and my band which matched Natu's band and Fatou gushed about the stylings and the cut of the stone. During our meal, everyone toasted us and gave us their well wishes. Mostly though, we talked about last night's celebration. Chief Anuna was the first to speak and he blessed our marriage and spoke about last night's event as well. He told us, "I'm a Chief, but my flock is small. I'm not used to speaking to a large group like we saw last night, but I made it through it. I was very proud of all of us. It reminded me that in many ways, we never really mourned our collective losses. We've been in defensive, reactionary stance for centuries, literally. Last night, we exhaled." We raised our glasses and toasted his remarks.

When we were done, Natu stood up, placed his arm around me and thanked everyone for attending. We could have lingered a little longer and enjoyed each other's company, but Natu was anxious to get to the hotel in Dakar and the men just kind of looked at each other and smiled. He grabbed my bag and we entered the car waiting for us to launch into our lifetime adventure as husband and wife.

A. YVONNE STOKES

By the Board of Directors and Honorary Elders of

Motherland Bound, Incorporated
Of the City of Phoenix and the State of Arizona,
United States of America

****

To all to whom these Presents shall come, Greetings:

Please Take Notice that I, *Patrice Simmons*, having applied to relocate my family to the continent of Africa from which I and my forbearers were unwillingly removed over Four Hundred years ago, and being a person of African ancestry **DO HEREBY RESOLVE** to re-claim my African heritage, and disavow and invalidate the false hypothesis that I am a member of a lost people with no discernable history or homeland.

I hereby proclaim enormous pride in my African ancestry and Quantify my worth by the measure of faith in the resurrection, which I was given by Almighty God, the most omnipotent, the all-powerful, the most omniscient, eternal and transcendent.

Patrice Simmons

Therefore, the Chair and fellow Board Member of Motherland Bound, with the consent of the Honorable and the Reverend Board of Elders, in solemn council assembled hereby declare Patrice Simmons a lifelong member of Motherland Bound.

In testimony whereof, authenticated by the Seal of Motherland Bound, Incorporated, SWORN TO and DATED this *29th* day of *March*, in the year of *2019*, **A.D. and the Motherland Bound year** *1.*

Signed by
Board of Directors
    The Elders

Karima Powers
    Chief Anuna
Fatou Diallo
    Elder Bunmi Whey
Kofi Diallo
    Elder Tamu
Simone Davies
    Elder Batu
Keith Mackie

ABOUT THE AUTHOR

A. Yvonne Stokes, first time author, grew up in Los Angeles, in a big, loving family. Like her main character, Karima, she earns a living and contributes to society but has longed to rebuild the lives of the disadvantaged by reason of poverty and discrimination. In writing "Karima's Journey Back to Africa," the author experienced a vicarious actualization of a life changing initiative that resets broken lives.

www.ingramcontent.com/pod-product-compliance
Lightning Source LLC
Chambersburg PA
CBHW051245250626
47155CB00009B/3166